Murder in Calico Gold

A Cedar Bay Cozy Mystery - Book 6

BY

DIANNE HARMAN

Published by: Dianne Harman
www.dianneharman.com

Interior, cover design and website by
Vivek Rajan Vivek
www.vivekrajanvivek.com

ISBN: 978-1514343272

CONTENTS

ACKNOWLEDGMENTS

Loyal readers, I can't thank you enough for making my books so popular! Five of the books in the Cedar Bay Cozy Mystery Series have been designated as "All-Star" books by Amazon based on their sales, and I also have been named as one of their most popular authors. None of this would have happened without you!

Many of you have emailed me to say how much you enjoy my books, as well as giving me suggestions for future books in this series. Trust me, I take each one of your suggestions very seriously. You've helped me grow as an author. I always appreciate reviews, and I'd love to hear from you about this book or any of my other books. Feel free to email me at: dianne@dianneharman.com.

If you like my book covers, and I'm constantly told by readers how much they do, Vivek Rajan deserves the kudos. He's also the fearless formatter who makes my books look good on the inside as well! Thanks, Vivek!

The encouragement of my family and friends has been critical to the success of my writing, but most of all, I have to thank Tom for reading and editing each chapter of my books. He tells me what works and what doesn't and makes suggestions. Guns are often in my books, and believe me, without his expertise, I would constantly be challenged in that area! Tom, thanks for your thoughts and never-ending encouragement! I know a lot of my success is due to you!

Lastly, I can't forget my six month old Boxer puppy, Kelly. I've told a number of people they should invest in a company that sells toilet paper, because her favorite thing to do is to get a roll of it when we forget to close a bathroom door and race down the stairs, ears flying, leaving a white trail behind her. One of my family members suggested I use it in a book – murderer caught after becoming tangled up in toilet paper. Who knows? You might just read about it!

Newsletter

To keep abreast with my latest releases kindly go to www.dianneharman.com and sign up for my newsletter. Thank you.

CHAPTER ONE

"Mike, when was the last time you saw your Aunt Agnes?" Kelly asked as they started the nine hour drive to Calico Gold from their home in Cedar Bay located on the Oregon coast. At the same time she looked in the back seat to make sure their dogs, Rebel and Lady, were comfortable for the long trip ahead of them.

"I think it was probably ten years or so," the big burly middle-aged sheriff said. "I kept meaning to drive down there, but you know how it is. You think you will and then something happens, and it's put on the back burner. We've always talked on the phone about once a week, so even though I didn't actually see her, I've always felt close to her."

"Since I've never met her, and she's really your only relative, I'd like to know more about her."

"When I was a young child I spent a lot of summers at her ranch, named the Robertson Ranch. It's in Calico Gold, which is a small town located in the foothills of the Sierra Nevada Mountains in Central California. Anyway, she has a huge, at least it was to me in my childhood days, old Victorian house called the Robertson House. The ranch and the house were named in honor of my great-grandmother whose maiden name was Robertson. Years ago my aunt and uncle ran cattle on the ranch which is pretty fair-sized, about a hundred and fifty acres. Aunt Agnes had several horses, and she was

1

still riding the last time I saw her. She would have been about seventy something then. There was a big old barn on the ranch where the horses were kept, and a small stream ran through the property. My aunt and uncle wanted to live off of the grid before it became a trendy thing to do, so they dammed up the stream and created a small lake. They used the water from it for their cattle and all of the other water needs of the ranch.

"When I was a kid I used to play in an abandoned shack that was next to the stream and pretend I was a cowboy. I had a horse I always rode when I visited, and Aunt Agnes even had a special saddle made just for me. It was so different from city living. I remember she had some pigs and chickens and lots of other things that are typically found on a ranch and are very interesting to a young boy from the city. Like I said, they wanted to live off the grid.

"I remember her as being quite opinionated and a real spitfire. She didn't mince words, and everyone knew exactly how she felt about a subject. She was kind of like a present-day civic activist. Aunt Agnes was an environmentalist before it became a commonly used household word. I know one of her neighbors wasn't happy when she dammed up the stream on her property because it stopped him from getting water, and for ranchers that can be critical. It's probably more critical now with the drought that California's been experiencing."

"She sounds really interesting. I'm curious why your grandparents gave the ranch to her and not your mother. After all, they were sisters and the only two children of your grandparents. That seems like kind of a strange thing to do."

"If you'd known my grandparents, it wouldn't seem very strange. They never approved of my father and were furious with my mother when she married him. Their way of retaliating was to give the ranch to Aunt Agnes. I remember hearing they were worried she'd be a spinster, so they wanted to take care of her. I've always given a great deal of credit to my mother for not being jealous of Aunt Agnes for getting the ranch. I never heard her say anything negative about it, and I know it must have hurt."

"I'm sorry I never met your mother. She sounds like a saint. Not too many sisters would react that way. I've never heard you mention cousins. Did Aunt Agnes have any children?"

"Yes, she had a son, Duncan. He was killed when he was in the service during the Vietnam War, really at the very end of the war. I know she and my uncle had a hard time dealing with it. I kind of remember she often let Vietnam vets live in the shack I told you about if they needed a place to stay. I don't know if she's still doing that."

"When she called you did she give you any indication why she wanted you to come to Calico Gold? Was she in trouble or ill health? What does she look like?"

"She told me she would tell me all about it when I got there. She mentioned she was involved in some controversial activities, and she might need my expertise as a lawman. I don't have a clue what she meant by that, and I have no idea what she wants, but I'm a little concerned. I asked her if her health was all right, and she said that wasn't why she wanted to see me. Aunt Agnes, in her typical way, was adamant she was in perfect health, although I have a little trouble believing someone who's got to be in her mid-80's is in perfect health.

"As far as what she looks like now, I don't know. I remember her as being a threatening looking type of woman. She was tall and had a ramrod straight posture. She wore glasses that were attached to a necklace so she wouldn't lose them. She always wore pants. I guess that was because she rode so much and was out on the ranch with the animals almost every day. I remember my mother kidding her about it, saying that she didn't have a feminine bone in her body, and she should have been a man."

"Wow! That's pretty harsh. Does she live by herself? If she's in her 80's, that's kind of getting up there in years to be living alone."

"Yes, she's lived alone in the Robertson House ever since Uncle Max passed away, and that's been over twenty years ago. She's never mentioned anyone else living in the house. I really don't know much about her personal life, but I guess we'll find out soon enough."

CHAPTER TWO

Ever since he'd arrived at the Roadhouse Bar some six hours earlier, Gary Sanders had been drinking steadily. He went to the bar every night and stayed until closing time at 2:00 a.m. After he finished his "last call" drink, he headed for the parking lot, unsteadily got on his motorcycle, and headed for home. He was temporarily living in a small shack located on the edge of the stream that ran through the Robertson Ranch. After his mother died, he'd been homeless. The shack, courtesy of Agnes Johnson, the owner of the Robertson Ranch and a friend of his mother's, provided some limited shelter for him. The shack had been a godsend, a place where he felt safe.

Twice after he'd left the Roadhouse Bar he'd woken up in the hospital, once with a skull fracture, and once with a broken leg. He'd fallen off his motorcycle after he'd been drinking. The voices in his head told him he could fly, but they'd been wrong. He never told the doctors in Vietnam he'd been hearing the voices ever since he was a little boy. The voices told him to do things, and he'd be fine. They'd always been wrong, but still he listened to them. They were so insistent, he didn't have a choice. He remembered the time when he was ten years old, and he'd been injured when he fell out of a tree. They'd told him he could easily jump to the ground.

The voices were the reason he'd enlisted in the Army when he turned eighteen. They told him he needed to go to Vietnam, and he'd be safe because the war was almost over. When he was in Vietnam he heard the voices a lot. One time he told an Army doctor about them, and he'd prescribed medicine for Gary to take. He told Gary the reason he heard the voices was because of the stress of being in Vietnam. The doctor was wrong. He started taking the medicine and the voices became quiet, but when he returned to Calico Gold after the war, they began whispering to him again, telling him bad things he should do. He tried not to listen, but it didn't help. People thought his strange behavior was a result of the time he'd spent in Vietnam. They didn't know the voices had been in Gary's head since he was a child.

When he returned from Vietnam his mother tried to get help for him, but her insurance didn't cover conditions related to mental health. She had very little money and what little money she did have went to support herself and Gary. She didn't have the money to hire expensive doctors or lawyers to plead with the county to have him committed or at least put under some type of a conservatorship. She'd even tried the Veterans Administration, but they were no help at all. She'd cared for him by herself until she'd died.

Gary had never really been in trouble with the law and although his behavior was strange, nothing he had done qualified him as being "mentally incompetent." He was in that grey area where help was almost impossible to find unless you were a person of means. His mother didn't have any money for a private mental institution, and anyway, the voices in his head told him he didn't need any help. After his mother passed away, there was no one who cared enough about him to try and have him committed to a mental institution, even if a bed had been available. His life consisted of a hand to mouth existence – doing odd jobs and buying food and alcohol with what he was paid. Gary wasn't capable of thinking about what the future held for him. His existence was bleak, and lately the voices in his head had been getting louder and more demanding.

It didn't seem strange to Gary that the voices told him it would be fun to see someone die. He'd seen a lot of death in Vietnam, and while he didn't consider it fun, it was a fact of daily life when you were in Nam. The voices told him maybe he should kill someone, because he'd really felt alive when he was killing people in Vietnam.

Gary had become amoral, if, in fact, he had ever had a sense of what was right and what was wrong.

He knew it was just a matter of time before he killed someone. The voices were going to get their way and he knew it. They always did.

CHAPTER THREE

"Wow," Kelly said as they left the highway and drove onto the main street of Calico Gold. "There's a little of everything here. Sierra Nevada Mountains in the background, all kinds of shops and names reflecting the gold mining history of the town, and restored old period buildings. Even though it looks like it gets a lot of tourists, the mark of the early settlers is definitely still here. I've never been to California's gold country, but I feel like I'm in it now."

"It's been many years since I've been here, but I have to admit it's not quite like I remember it. Looks to me like they've had some outside money come in and make everything pretty for the tourists. The people I remember from here didn't have that kind of money, and if they did, that's not how they would have spent it," Mike said.

"I did a little research on the town last night when you were working late. Did you notice that bed and breakfast located on the edge of town? It's called the Gold Dust Bed and Breakfast Inn, and it opened a few years ago. Evidently a couple from San Francisco wanted to get away from big city living and bought ten acres of land with an old barn on it. They renovated the barn and kept adding to it until they had a rustic inn. The article said people come from all over California and the Northwest to stay there. It's got gardens and a koi pond, plus the rooms are supposed to be really well-decorated. However, I have to agree with you, while it looks sort of rustic, it definitely has a big city feel to it."

"See that restaurant over there, Lucky Luke's? I remember my aunt and uncle would bring me into town as a special treat, and we'd go there to have hamburgers and chocolate malted milks. It had a sawdust floor, and there were bowls of peanuts on all of the wooden tables. Everybody threw their peanut shells on the floor. The reason it really stuck in my mind is because I knew my mother would never let me do that at home, so it was a real treat."

Kelly laughed, "Nor would mine. We told your aunt we'd be there about 6:00, and we're a little early. Let's walk the dogs, stop at Lucky Luke's, and see if it's still the same."

A few minutes later Mike opened the front door of the restaurant and stood still, looking at the eatery in amazement. The sawdust had been replaced by shiny terra cotta tiles. The old scarred wooden bar that had run the length of one wall had been replaced with a sleek marble top bar, its color matching the tile floor. Multi-colored boutique tequila bottles were set against a mirrored back wall behind the bar. On both ends of the wall were lists of the specialty beers they sold.

"I can't believe this," Mike said. "It's like someone has completely trashed my wonderful childhood memories. You probably can't even get a hamburger anymore."

"Well, we're here. Let's sit down, have a beer, and look at the menu. Might be interesting. Who knows, I might even get some ideas for Kelly's Koffee Shop." The hostess showed them to a window table that looked out on Main Street.

"When we used to come here the only vehicles on Main Street were trucks. That's all anybody drove. Look at it now. I can see a Mercedes, a Bentley, and a Lexus. So much for small town life."

"Mike, you won't believe this menu. This is as good as anything you'd find in San Francisco or Portland. I mean, what small town restaurant features lobster bisque and a seasonal vegetable pizza? Plus a whole section of the menu is devoted to gourmet cheese plates that they have available. I've never even heard of Truffle Tremor cheese."

"Something is definitely going on here in Calico Gold. When we drove down the street, there were still some old buildings I remember from years ago. They don't look any different, but there are also the new ones like this restaurant that must be catering to wealthy people from San Francisco and other big cities. Be willing to bet there's a big division between the old-timers who probably want to keep things just like they've always been and the ones who are willing to put a lot of money into some of these places, hoping to attract even bigger money. I can just imagine how Aunt Agnes feels about it. Knowing her and her dislike for change, I'm sure she's not happy about this. I can't say I blame her. If they do much more, the town will begin to resemble Napa. I have to say I don't like these changes."

"This isn't quite what I expected," Kelly said." I was looking for a sleepy little town with some colorful grizzled looking old retired gold miners wearing suspenders and cowboy boots. I'm really curious to talk to your aunt and find out what's happening."

"Drink up. Time for you to meet Aunt Agnes," Mike said as he motioned the waitress over and asked for the check.

Later, Kelly wished they'd spent that hour with Aunt Agnes instead of at Lucky Luke's. Their time with her was cut short by unexpected events. Events like murder.

CHAPTER FOUR

I can't believe she's going to give the ranch to my cousin, the cousin I've never met. I should be the one to have it for what her family did to Mother and me.

Daniel Noonan was a tall lean man with grey shoulder length hair and a matching mustache. He went into the kitchen, took a bottle of bourbon out of the cabinet, poured himself a stiff drink and then walked into the living room of the cabin his aunt had bought for him. He paused for a moment, looking at the paintings that lined the walls, his paintings. He knew they didn't appeal to most people who only wanted to see flowers or oceans or landscapes. Daniel preferred to paint what he saw in his mind. Several gallery owners had told him his paintings were too dark and disturbing, and they refused to exhibit his work.

I know they're dark, but if people had the childhood and life I've had, they'd paint the darkness too. There were no pretty things in my life when I was growing up.

He took a large slug from the glass of bourbon he held in his hand and thought back to his childhood. He remembered how he'd been teased for never having a father come to any of his school events. Some of the other kids didn't have fathers attend the events because their parents were divorced, but he'd never even had a father. For that matter, when he was young he never knew he had a relative other than his mother. Daniel had never forgiven his mother's parents for not allowing any contact between him and other family members. When his mother was dying of cancer she'd told him about the family members he'd never met, and about the same time she'd asked Agnes, her sister, to look after him when she was gone. He felt it was about time somebody from the family paid some attention to him. He felt no guilt whatsoever about the cabin and the money that was being given to him every month by Aunt Agnes. Daniel felt it was long overdue, and she could easily do much more for him.

Daniel visited his aunt once a month for dinner. If anyone were to ask him he would tell them that he and his aunt were very close, and that they had dinner at her house every month. What he wouldn't tell them was the only reason he went there was to get the monthly "allowance" she gave him. In his mind he always referred to her as "the old biddy."

His needs were few, and the money Aunt Agnes gave him covered his expenses. Agnes had bought the cabin for him outright. When he realized how large the ranch and the house were, he was sure his luck was finally going to change. Daniel knew he had a cousin. His aunt had told him all about Mike Reynolds, how he was the sheriff of Beaver County, Oregon, and had just married a woman who had two grown children and owned a successful coffee shop in Cedar Bay, Oregon.

What he never expected was that he would be left out of his aunt's Will and her entire estate would be left to his cousin, Mike Reynolds. He still couldn't believe what his aunt had told him about the terms of her Will at dinner the other night. In his mind the house and the ranch were his rightful inheritance. The thought that he would inherit it seemed absolutely fair to him. He was surprised she hadn't asked him to move onto the property a long time ago. What did an old biddy like her need all that land and house for? No, it absolutely made no sense at all. The right thing would be to give it to Daniel. After all, Agnes had inherited it from her parents, and her parents were the reason his mother had to work two jobs to support them and save for him to go to college. It never occurred to him that maybe it was time for him to take care of himself. First his mother had taken care of him, and now his aunt had assumed the responsibility of caring for him.

The more he thought about the cousin he'd never met, Mike Reynolds, inheriting the property, the madder he got. His aunt had effectively dashed his dreams, and she should pay for it. The corners of his mouth turned up in a sinister smile as a plan slowly began to develop in his mind.

CHAPTER FIVE

After they left Lucky Luke's, Mike said, "Kelly, I've got to get some gas for the car. I had no idea it was almost on empty. There used to be a gas station about a block away. I'll see if it's still there."

Kelly and Mike saw the old gas station at the same moment. "Mike, this is like a step back into the past. I haven't seen a station like this in years."

They stared in amazement, taking in the stone building with the two yellow pumps out in front. An American flag fluttered in the breeze on a pole next to the pumps. There was a little office on the left side of the building and a garage on the right. The windows didn't look like they'd ever been washed and were yellow with age. Mike pulled in next to one of the pumps, got out of the car, filled the gas tank and walked into the little office.

"Be $48.24," the old man with leathery skin and a full white beard said as he took a deep drag from the cigarette anchored between his lips.

That's why I couldn't see in the windows. They're not yellow with age but with smoke from his cigarettes.

He raised his head and peered at Mike through his bifocals. "Son, you look kinda familiar. From around these parts?"

14

"No. I'm visiting my aunt, Agnes Johnson. She lives about a mile out of town."

"Now I remember ya'. Yer' Agnes' nephew. Ya' used to come in here with yer' aunt and uncle when ya' were visitin' for the summer. What brings ya' here now?" he asked.

"I'm sorry, but I don't remember your name."

"Name's Ralph, same as it's been forever. So yer' Agnes' nephew. Ya' come to help her or what?"

"Help her with what?" Mike asked.

"Try to keep her property. Coupla' people want it real bad. John Wilson, the rancher south of her property wants it for water, and some out-of-town developer wants to put a golf course on it."

"You've got to be kidding! A golf course on the Robertson Ranch? Well, I don't know anything about that. She called me the other day and asked me to come down here. She said she had some things she wanted to talk to me about. I recently remarried, and Aunt Agnes couldn't make it to the wedding, so my wife and I decided to visit her."

"She could probably use some help from ya'. She's got her thinkin' in the right place, unlike a lot of these newbies in town. Actually, she's kind of a living legend in this town."

"Ralph, what's happened to Calico Gold? I remember it as a sleepy little town, but it sure doesn't look that way now."

"Ya' got that right. Big money comin' in here. Ya' probably saw that fancy schmancy bed and breakfast on the outskirts of town and some of the others. Got some people here who wanna make Calico Gold into 'nother Napa. Lots of wineries around these parts, even made some of the old gold mines into tasting rooms. Them rich investors figger all the big spenders from places like San Francisco will come here and go wine tasting. Pretty soon I'll bet there'll be a T-shirt shop selling shirts that say 'I tasted golden wine in Calico Gold.'

"There's a bunch of us that don't like it. Yer' aunt's one of 'em. Big bucks wanted me to, what's the word, oh yeah, modernize my gas station. Said it was too old fashioned. Told 'em to stick their nose in someone else's bizness, that I wasn't doin' nothin' of the kind. Like this old station just as it is, I do. Me and it been through a lot together."

"I like it too. It brings back a lot of old memories. So who's behind all of these changes? You keep referring to them as big bucks. Got any names?"

"They ain't never had the courage to say who's behind it. Kind of smoke and mirrors. Who knows? Maybe a coupla' people here in Calico Gold wanted to get rich and approached some investors from San Francisco or Los Angeles." He was interrupted by the roar of a motorcycle traveling at a high rate of speed down Main Street.

"What the heck? That's something I never saw in Calico Gold when I was visiting. Speeding motorcycles. Is that one of the tourists?"

"Nah. That's Gary Sanders. He's a Vietnam vet who lives in that shack on yer' aunt's property. When he came back from Nam he lived with his mother, Jessica, in her house. She died, and he found out she'd been renting the house. Didn't have no money or a job, so yer' aunt said he could live in the shack on her property that's next to the stream. Yer' aunt and his mother, Jessica, were real close."

"I knew she used to let some of the vets live there while they got back on their feet."

"I'd say she's a soft touch. That Gary's a bad apple. Came back from Nam and was never the same. Got a big ol' mean streak in him and a temper that would make a junk yard dog look like a cuddly little puppy. Gets liquored up, and all he wants to do is fight. Can't tell ya' how many times he's been kicked out of the Roadhouse Bar. Think everyone in town would like to see him leave."

"Does he help my aunt around the ranch?"

"She says he does. Don't think so. These days she leases out almost all of her ranch to a coupla' local ranchers who run cattle on it. Not much for him to do. Might muck the horse stall once in a while, but that's 'bout it. She pays a coupla' people from the church to go out to her house and clean it every week. Yer' aunt's still driving the old pickup she's had for years, and she's got that big dog she always brings with her when she comes to town."

"Ralph, I don't want to be late to my aunt's. Thanks for the information. See you later."

"Somethin' I can do fer ya' or yer' aunt, let me know. Glad yer' here. She can use ya'." He gave Mike a half salute and looked out the window at the Lexus that had pulled in behind Mike's car. He shook his head. "Don't that take all? See what I'm talkin' 'bout?"

"Yeah, I sure do. I'll see you in a few days."

On the way to the ranch he told Kelly about his conversation with Ralph.

"Wonder if that's why she wanted you to come for a visit."

"Don't know sweetheart, but we'll find out in a few minutes," he said as he turned down the lane that led to the Robertson Ranch.

CHAPTER SIX

It had not been an easy day for Judge Susan Lane. Difficult attorneys, cases where the law was hazy, and a frantic call from Richard Martin, all added to her stress. She'd told Richard she'd call him tonight. She knew what he wanted. She'd been promising him she could do something about the Agnes Johnson situation, but she wasn't exactly sure what she was going to do.

Agnes was not only refusing to sell her property to Richard or even to meet with him to look at the plans the golf course architect had made, but she was also funding Huston Brooks in his campaign to unseat Susan in the upcoming election. Susan knew the judge's race might be close, but as an incumbent she felt she had the edge. With regard to the Agnes Johnson situation, Richard had promised her if she could get Agnes to sell him the property, he could make enough off of it to be able to afford to divorce his wife and marry Susan, but time was running out. She looked at the phone and then poured herself a glass of wine, nervously running her fingernail, painted fire engine red, around the rim of the glass.

Might as well get this over with, although I know pretty much what he's going to say. He's going to want to know what I've done about Agnes, and that hasn't been much.

"Richard, it's Susan," she said a moment later. "Sorry I couldn't talk when you called earlier, but I was in the middle of a difficult situation in court. The defense and the prosecution attorneys were about to come to blows, and I was trying to mediate it. How are you tonight?"

"Sounds like you had a bad day. Sorry, but time's beginning to run out on this Agnes Johnson property. My financial backers are getting antsy, and I want to know exactly what you have in mind, so I can reassure them that the golf course will be built. Don't forget that I'm backing your re-election. What's the status?"

"I'm in a bit of a difficult position myself," Susan said. "You know I can make sure you get all of the easements, entitlements, and other things you need, but my opponent in the upcoming race for my judge's seat is being funded by Agnes Jonson. He's very anti-development and wants to keep Calico Gold just the way it is. He's completely opposed to a golf course being built on her property. Naturally I'm not number one on her list of people she wants to do things for."

"Frankly, Susan, even though I promised I'd get you the funds needed for your campaign, I have to tell you I really don't care about your judge's seat. We have an agreement, and you need to keep your end of the deal. If I'm going to divorce Denise, that property has to be developed. And if that property isn't developed, I'm going to have to stay with Denise. It's as simple as that. If I were to get divorced without it being developed, Denise would get the majority of our assets, because a good attorney would make a case that Denise's inheritance provided the funding for most of our assets. That would be true and believe me, she has the documentation to prove it. Matter of fact, I would be darned near penniless, and I don't think you want to marry a man who's penniless. Your champagne tastes would have to come down a few notches. Don't think you'd like shopping for your St. John knit suits on eBay rather than at Nordstrom's in San Francisco."

"I've been thinking a lot about this, Richard, and I have a plan. You're simply going to have to trust me. This is probably one of those times that the less you know about something, the better off you're going to be."

"All right, Susan. You know the landscape there better than I do, but let me make it very clear to you that something needs to be done and sooner rather than later. I can't wait much longer. I'm going to tell my financial backers that we should be able to get the property in about a month. Make sure you meet that requirement, or that will be the end of the Lane-Martin relationship."

"I promise, Richard. Agnes Johnson will not be a problem in a very short time. You can tell your backers that."

"Thanks, sweetheart. I knew I could count on you. Just think what it will be like when we're together all the time. All that's standing in our way is Agnes Johnson, and if you're unable to take care of the situation, I will. Do I make myself clear?"

"Yes, I understand. I'll talk to you in a few days."

Now I just need to find someone to carry out my plan, Susan thought as she reached for her glass of wine.

*****

Richard ended the call and wondered if Susan would be able to deliver on her promise. If not, he would have to take things into his own hands. He'd give her twenty-four hours. That was it. He couldn't afford to wait any longer. It wouldn't be the first time he'd done something that didn't adhere to the letter of the law, but it was the first time he'd ever contemplated eliminating someone so he could have what he wanted.

Stupid woman. She's putty in my hands. Like I'd marry a small town judge who looks as cheap as she does with her brassy dyed hair and skirts that are several inches too short. Don't think she's familiar with the word "class." Denise may have her problems, but she definitely has class. Susan's the key to sidestepping a lot of the technicalities involved with developing a property like the Robertson Ranch, but Susan as a wife? Don't think so. I have far bigger plans than marrying Susan Lane of Calico Gold, but I'll continue to play her like a fish on the line until I get this project built.

He smiled, thinking how smart he'd been to figure out how he could get around the technicalities and zoning regulations involved in converting an old historic ranch into a golf course. A lonesome judge was his answer, but it was only a short-term answer. He knew if she wasn't able to produce what he needed, he'd have to resort to some rather unsavory measures.

CHAPTER SEVEN

"Mike, the house is huge! Even though you're over 6' 2", you're still going to feel small in it, just like when you were a kid. Actually, it's one of the most beautiful Victorian homes I've ever seen. Look at it. She's really kept it up. That's unusual for someone to do when they're in their 80's."

Mike stopped the car at the end of the lane, and they both spent a moment looking at the beautiful old house. "My great-grandparents bought the ranch and built the house in 1902. From what my mother told me, Victorian homes were all the rage in those days. You can see that it's a three story house, and I used to imagine there were ghosts staring at me from all those windows on the top floor. Aunt Agnes told me it was known as a Queen Anne home because of the number of turrets and the large wrap-around porch. I can remember sitting out there with my aunt and uncle at night while my uncle pointed out the stars and named them for me. My aunt told me her grandparents made a lot of money in the gold rush, and they wanted to build a house which reflected their status. This house certainly did."

"Oh, Mike, it's simply charming. I can't imagine how long it must have taken to build it. It has a number of different kinds of designs and styles of windows. It's so unique it should be preserved for future generations."

"I agree. If what Ralph said is true and someone wants to buy the property and make it into a golf course, I sure hope they'll preserve this house."

The front door opened just as Mike stopped their car on the circular driveway in front of the house, and a tall woman in jeans with her white hair pulled back in a bun came down the front steps, followed by a tri-colored collie dog with a coat that looked like it had just been brushed.

"Mike, I'm so glad to see you. Thank you for coming. Welcome to the Robertson House," she said as she put her arms around both of them. She stepped back and said, "You must be Kelly. Mike told me you were beautiful, but that doesn't do you justice," she said to the dark haired full figured woman who wore her hair pulled back and held by a tortoise shell clip, her large green eyes sparkling with intelligence.

"Thank you very much. I'm so glad to finally have the chance to meet you. Mike speaks so highly of you."

"We had some good times here when he was younger. This is my friend, Sam. You haven't met him Mike, he's the latest in the long line of collies we've had for years. You're probably tired, so let me show you to your room, and then you can come downstairs, and we'll have dinner. You probably want to rest for a little while, so take your time. I've got a leg of lamb in the oven with some roasted vegetables and some apricot bread. Hope that's all right with you."

"Sounds wonderful, Agnes, but if you have time I'd love a quick tour of the property and the house. It's one of the most beautiful I've ever seen," Kelly said.

"Of course. Let me know when you're ready," Agnes said as she opened a door that led to a suite of rooms on the second floor. "The bathroom is through that door, and there's a television and couch in the room on the other side of that door. Interestingly enough, my grandparents put a financial provision in their Will that allowed future generations to keep up the house, so I've always been able to bring in the latest things, like these light dimmers. The bathrooms and kitchen have been upgraded several times, so I think you'll be happy with your accommodations. I'll see you in a little while."

Kelly opened the bathroom door. "Mike, I've only seen bathrooms like this one in pictures of five star hotels. Good grief! I can't even imagine what this must have cost."

"Come in here," he said from the room on the far side of the suite. "You're not going to believe this." The room was a mixture of early 20th century antiques and plush modern chairs and couches. A state of the art giant screen television was mounted on the wall. An antique roll-top desk occupied one wall and plaid club chairs flanked the large window which overlooked the back of the ranch.

"I'm going downstairs. I've got to have the tour. Does it look different than you remember?" Kelly asked.

"I thought it would be much smaller and none of these latest touches like the television or the jets in the wall of the tiled shower were here. I think I need to take the tour as well."

CHAPTER EIGHT

While driving back to town after ending his long meeting with John Wilson, Richard Martin looked at his watch and was surprised to see it was already 6:00 p.m. Richard had presented his offer to buy John's ranch, and once again John had turned him down.

Fool keeps hoping that old widow, Agnes Johnson, will open up her dam so he can get water. From everything I've heard, she has no intention of ever doing that. Probably wouldn't be much fun to watch all your cattle die of thirst. Well, at least I'll be able to get his property when that happens. What I need is the Robertson Ranch. If I could get that, I'd have some leverage over John, because he knows I'd develop it, and there never would be a chance for him to get water from that stream. I'd stock that lake with fish and make money off of it.

Richard saw the neon lights of the Roadhouse Bar up ahead and decided to stop for a beer and a hamburger. He parked his car and entered the dimly lit cowboy bar that had served thirsty travelers, gold miners, and cowboys for over a century. An old-fashioned jukebox in the corner was playing a Johnny Cash song about prison life. Richard knew it was illegal to smoke in a place that served food, but from the hazy atmosphere, it was apparent nobody enforced the law.

He sat down at the bar and stood out like a blinking red beacon in his three piece pin stripe suit and polished cordovan shoes. He looked around and decided this was not a place to order a Sauvignon Blanc glass of wine. The grizzled, bearded bartender, who had the muscled body of a bouncer, walked over to him and asked, "What'll you have?"

"Give me a Sierra Nevada in the bottle."

"Ya' kiddin, right? Everybody here gets their beer in a bottle. Ain't got none of them fancy what do you call 'em, steins. We jes' got bottles here."

"Sounds good."

The bartender put the bottle of beer in front of Richard. "Don't much look like ya' belong around here. From Frisco?"

"Yes."

"What brings ya' out our way?"

"I'm trying to buy a couple of ranches and develop them."

"Whose ya' got in mind, if ya' don't mind me askin'?"

"Don't mind at all. I've been talking to John Wilson, and I'm trying to talk to Agnes Johnson."

"Long as Wilson has his cattle and he can get water, he won't sell to ya'. Ranch has been in the family too long. As fer Agnes, ain't no way she'd sell that ranch for developin'. She's got more nerve than Carter has little liver pills, and she's just as stubborn."

"That's what I keep hearing."

"Ya' see that wild-eyed guy at the end of the bar? One with all the tats? Might wanna' talk to him. He lives on her property."

Richard looked down the bar in the direction the bartender had nodded. A heavily tattooed man with shoulder length grey hair was seated at the end of the bar. Even though it was early in the evening, from the sound of the man's voice, Richard could tell it wasn't the first beer he'd had. He looked back at the bartender, "Does he come here often?"

"Every night. Sometimes in the afternoons if he's not workin'. Today's one of those times. Been here for a few hours. Coupla times had to kick him out. Always stays 'til closin' time if he's got any money. Sometimes the brewskies make him real mean. Been in a few fights I've had to break up."

"He doesn't seem like the kind of man Agnes Johnson would have living on her ranch. Is he a relative or something?"

"Nah. Everyone knows she's got a soft spot for vets that served in Nam. Her son died in the Vietnam War, so a lot of them have lived in that shack over the years. Gary," he motioned to the man at the bar, "is jes' the latest one. His mother was a friend of Agnes'."

"How does he support himself?"

"Doin' anything he can. Gets a little money from an odd job here and there, and then comes in here and drinks 'til it's gone. Always needin' money. Spends what he makes, but he don't make much."

A plan began to take form in Richard's mind. "I think I'll go over and talk to him. Had a brother who was in Nam. Thanks for telling me about him, and you can bring me another beer and give him one as well."

He walked to the end of the bar and took a seat on the bar stool next to Gary, as the bartender put beers in front of Gary and Richard.

"Whoa. Better put that one back in the cooler. Didn't order it. I'm out of money for tonight," Gary said.

"It's on me. My name is Richard Martin. Bartender says your name is Gary. Got a last name?"

"Thanks. Yeah, last name's Sanders. How come yer' buyin'?" he said, slightly slurring his words and looking warily at Richard.

"I had a brother who was in Nam. Any time I can do something for a vet, I do it. Shame what this country did to you and yours."

"Yep. You can say that again. Where did your brother serve?"

"He was in Da Nang. Bad place to be."

"Yeah, know it well. Too well."

"I understand you're living on the Robertson Ranch. Isn't that owned by some old woman?"

"Yeah, but I gotta find somewhere new to live when I get a little money. Old broad told me I had to leave. Problem is, I don't have anywhere to go. Just wish I had some money."

"So, what's she like? I hear she's pretty old."

"She's old, and she owns that ranch and that big house. More house and property than anyone should have. I don't know why she's kicking me out. Never did nothin' to deserve it, and I got nowhere to go. Old as she is, probably time for her to die."

Could be, my friend. It just could be.

"Maybe I can help you, and you can help me. I really don't want to talk business here, but how about if I meet you at your place tomorrow morning? I'd just as soon Agnes didn't see us meeting. Let's do it really early, say 5:00 a.m. I'll make if financially worthwhile for you."

"If I can make some money, I'll do it. There are two roads that go onto the ranch property. The first one goes to the Robertson House. Take the second one and go to the end. You'll see the shack I live in, and you can walk to it from there."

"Thanks," Richard said putting a twenty dollar bill on the bar and motioning to the bartender. "Keep the change and give Gary another beer," he said. He turned to Gary, "See you in the morning. I'm bringing someone with me. I'd just as soon you keep our meeting between us, so don't tell anyone about it. Need a ride home?"

"Nah. Got my wheels out in the parking lot. Old Bessie. She's a trustworthy hog. We've gone down a coupla times but always manage to stand back up. Wouldn't trade her for anything."

"Well, after our talk, you might be able to afford a new Bessie. Good night Gary, see you in the morning."

Richard got in his Lexus and made a U-turn in the parking lot while he called Susan Lane. "Susan, I've had a change of plans. I know when we talked earlier I said I had to get back to San Francisco tonight, but I've decided to spend the night. By the way, we have an appointment at 5:00 a.m. tomorrow morning. I think I've found the answer to our problem with Agnes Johnson. See you in a few minutes."

He ended the call and smiled, thinking how clever he was to find the answer to the Agnes Johnson problem.

CHAPTER NINE

Following the directions Gary Sanders had given him the night before when he met Gary at the Roadhouse Bar, Richard Martin quietly eased his silver Lexus down the lane that led to the shack where Gary lived. He'd spent the night at Judge Susan Lane's home, and as the new day dawned, he felt optimistic and refreshed. The plan he wanted to put into motion seemed like an ideal solution to the problem he was having with Agnes Johnson, the owner of the Robertson Ranch.

One way or the other, I've got to get rid of that old woman. Given the right inducement and a little encouragement, I'm sure Gary Sanders might just be my ticket to success, Richard thought as he brought the Lexus to a stop at the end of the lane.

It was 5:00 a.m. in the morning, and sunrise was only minutes away. The predawn sky was slowly turning to light grey from the deep darkness of night. Visibility was somewhat limited, but Richard could easily see the shack and the outhouse which stood next to it.

Susan was sitting in the front seat next to him. He turned to her and said, "There's the shack, right where he said it would be. I can see a glimmer of light coming from the only window in the place. Let's walk down there and see if we can convince Gary to do us a little favor. Remember what I told you last night about letting me do most of the talking. Your presence here is simply to convince Gary that if anything goes wrong with my plan, you'll be able to help him if he winds up in court."

They walked down the narrow dirt path that led to the shack, and Richard knocked on the door which was immediately opened by Gary. "Well I see you found my place and you're right on time," Gary said as he stepped aside and motioned for his two visitors to enter the shack.

The scene that met their eyes when they entered the shack was surreal. The shack was illuminated by a single Coleman lantern that sat hissing and sputtering on a makeshift bench that apparently served as a desk, work bench, and dining table, all rolled into one. Empty beer bottles and cans littered the floor and table. Fast food containers were scattered on the floor and everywhere else in the shack. In one corner was a small iron bed frame covered with a thin mattress and several filthy blankets. The shack had no electricity, running water, or a bathroom. A plastic five-gallon water bottle was propped up on a shelf on the far side of the shack and was evidently used to provide water for drinking and personal hygiene, the latter of which was completely lacking based on Gary's personal appearance.

Noticing the look of disbelief on the faces of his two visitors as they looked around the simple one room shack, Gary said, "Yeah, I know it ain't much of a place to live in, but it's all I got, and if things go as expected, this time next week I won't even have this 'cause the old lady who owns the ranch wants to kick me out. Claims me, my motorcycle, and my friends are all undesirables. So, Mr. Big Shot moneyman, what's so important that it brings you out here to my little 'ol run-down shack at this ungodly time in the morning? This better be good, and it better involve me gettin' some money out of it."

"I think it will, Gary, I think it will," Roger said, "but first let me introduce you to a good friend of mine, Judge Susan Lane." Susan extended her hand and she and Gary shook hands. "Susan's jurisdictional area includes Calico Gold and all the surrounding area. Any type of legal case, whether it's civil or criminal, eventually winds up in her courtroom. As I said, she's a good friend, and someone who can provide a huge amount of help if a person has a little run-in with the law.

"Before I get into the details of how we might be able to help each other, and at the same time make some serious money for you, I'd like to know a little more about you. I know you served a tour of duty in Vietnam, and I'm particularly interested in what you did while you were there. How about filling me in with some of those details?"

"Sure, I don't mind telling you about my time in Nam, since it totally screwed up my life and left me living like a dog in this disgusting little shack with no money and nowhere to go. I think about Nam and what it did to me every single waking moment of every day, and it makes me depressed and really angry. Added to that is the fact that the Veterans Administration won't do a thing for me and has left me high and dry with no benefits whatsoever. Suppose that's why I drink so much and get into fights. It's like I'm trying to wash away all those terrible memories of my time in Nam. So yeah, here's a quick sketch of what went down when I was there.

"When I arrived there I was assigned to the 4th Infantry Division in the central highlands. I was a combat infantryman, and my unit's job was to seek out the enemy and destroy him. We went into the field for weeks at a time carrying out what were called search and destroy missions. When we'd find a village where we thought the Viet Cong were being hidden, we'd shoot and kill every man, woman and child in the village and then burn it to the ground. Know it sounds pretty brutal, but it's what we did. All the brass hat generals and colonels in headquarters wanted to know was whether or not we'd cleared the area of the enemy and secured it. They didn't care how we did it, and they didn't ask any questions. I'm not proud I did it, but I sort of enjoyed it while I was doing it.

"All my life I've heard voices in my head telling me what to do, and when I was in Nam they told me what I was doing was the right thing to do. I probably killed more people in Nam than are buried in Calico Gold's cemetery. When I got out of the Army and came back here to Calico Gold my depression and anger started to get really bad. The little voices in my head liked it when I was killing innocent people in Nam, and they started urging me to do the same here in the States. It's pretty hard to control what the voices tell me to do. That's the background on me, and a little bit about what's going on in my head. Now why don't you tell me about yourself and most importantly, how I can make some money."

Richard paused for a moment and then slowly started to speak, "Gary, you and I each have a problem with Agnes Johnson, the owner of the Robertson Ranch. I'm a developer and want to buy the ranch and convert it into a golf course, but Agnes won't sell it to me or for that matter even talk to me. Your problem with her is she wants to kick you out of your home and turn you out on the street. I think it would be to our mutual benefit if something nasty happened to her. If she was gone, I'd be able to buy the ranch, and if I did, I guarantee you that you could continue to live here in the shack as long as you want. Everybody knows that working on a ranch can be dangerous and it seems like accidents on ranches happen all the time. A person can get kicked in the head by a horse or fall out of the hayloft in the barn and fracture their skull. You name it, but the fact of the matter is that serious accidents happen a lot around ranches. I'm thinking it would be nice if Agnes Johnson had a really serious accident. If she did, you and I would both benefit from it.

"I'll leave it up to you to think about what I just said and decide if there's anything you can do about it. Thanks for taking the time to meet with Judge Lane and me this morning. I promised you last night I'd make it worth your time if you'd meet with me, so here's an envelope that has $500 in unmarked small bills in it. It's yours to keep, no questions asked. Once I get ownership of this ranch, I've got another envelope with $5,000 in it that has your name written on the outside.

"It's almost light outside, and Judge Lane and I have to be going before someone spots us here. Again thanks for meeting with us. I think this may be the start of a profitable relationship for both of us, and remember, if anything goes wrong, Judge Lane will be able to help you out."

Roger and Susan left the shack and walked back to his car. As he drove back to the highway Roger failed to notice someone walking along the side of the lane.

CHAPTER TEN

There was a knock on John Wilson's office door, and it was opened by Les Scott, his ranch manager. "Les, how was your day? What's new?"

The weathered lean, lanky cowhand stood in front of John's desk, twirling his worn grey cowboy hat in his hands, a piece of chaw puffing out his right cheek. "John, we've been together a long time, but I gotta tell ya' I'm really worried. Had some guy come out today and measure how much water we've got left. Ain't good. He figures there's about enough water fer the cattle fer another three months. After that, unless there's a huge storm or we get water from somewhere else, we're finished. There won't be no more water."

John sat quietly for a few moments, his head in his hands. He looked up at Les. "I don't know what to do. Do you have any ideas?"

"None that we ain't already discussed. Best bet still seems to be from the stream that's on the Johnson property right next to us. Ya' gotta convince Mrs. Johnson to either open the dam she and her husband built quite a few years back or else sell the property to us. Don't think there's anything else we can do. Don't much believe in prayin', but this sure might be the time to do it. Also don't believe much in divine intervention, but maybe it'll happen. Maybe pigs'll fly to. That's where we're at."

"You make it sound imminent."

"John, ya' can't fool yourself any longer. If we don't get the water, the cattle will die, and ya' won't have no ranch. Ya' might be better off to sell it to that developer who's so hot to buy it. That or talk to Mrs. Johnson again."

"All right," he said, struggling to keep his voice from showing how afraid he was that he was going to lose the family ranch. "Thanks for letting me know. I'll come up with something. Don't worry."

"John, maybe it's time to let go. All things have to come to an end sooner or later. Don't mean ya' ain't tried yer best. You've done as good at keepin' this ranch as anyone. Don't blame yerself for what's happening. Drought wasn't caused by you. It was Mother Nature or some kind of a global warmin' thing. See ya' tomorrow. Try and get some sleep tonight. Maybe an answer'll come to ya' in a dream."

After Les had gone, John pushed himself out of his chair and began to pace the length of his office with heavy footsteps, back and forth, trying to think of some way he could save the ranch.

It's been in the family for over a century. There was plenty of water in the past, and we even used to get water from the stream on Agnes Johnson's property. I have to convince her to open the dam or sell her property to me.

He thought back to all the times over the years when he'd approached her to do one or the other, but her answer was always the same. She had no intention of selling the property, and she refused to open the dam because she had made a promise to her late husband, Max, to not rely on others, and that included city water.

John stopped at the far end of the room, taking a moment to look at the paintings of the Wilson men who had ranched on the property, starting with his great-grandfather. He knew what they must think of him – a man who couldn't keep the ranch in the family. What kind of a man was he? Generations of Wilsons had lived and prospered on this property. What kind of a man lets the property go to strangers? He turned away from the paintings, not wanting to see what to him looked like disgust in their eyes.

He was at the end of his rope. There was nothing to be gained by going to Agnes Johnson, hat in hand, literally, and begging her for mercy one more time. She was never going to open the dam or sell him the property. A thought that had flittered in the back of his mind for months made itself known, and he let it flow into his current thinking. He had always played by the rules and had never broken a law or even thought about it. What he was now thinking and planning was way beyond a simple infraction of the law. He knew if the police discovered it was him, he'd go to prison for life and lose the ranch. It was a gamble. He grimly decided he had to try it to save the ranch. He had to gamble that the police would never discover it was him.

Finally at peace with having made the decision, and knowing there was none other, he opened the door and walked to the kitchen to join his three sons and his wife for dinner. His sons' legacy was in his hands. He would do whatever was necessary to protect that legacy.

CHAPTER ELEVEN

"We're ready for the tour," Mike said as he and Kelly walked into the kitchen. "Aunt Agnes, you briefly introduced us to your friend, Sam, but it wasn't very formal. He looks exactly like Rudy, the collie you had the last time I was here."

"Probably does. Your uncle and I got started with this breed when we took over the ranch, and as soon as a dog started getting old, we'd get another puppy. There's a breeder not too far from here who we've been buying from for years. When your uncle was alive and we had a lot of cattle, we used the dogs for herding them. Since he's been gone I've always had one as a pet. Like I told you, his name is Sam. Don't have a clue why I named him that. Just seemed to fit. Let's get going. I don't want to overcook that lamb."

A half hour later, walking back to the main house from the barn, Kelly said, "I find it amazing you're living here all by yourself, except for Sam. This not only is a lot of land, it's a lot of house for one person."

"I'm used to it, and I like the solitude. Gary, a Vietnam vet that I've befriended, lives in that shack down by the stream, and if I ever need anything, I ask him to get it for me. I usually go into town about once a week to get any other supplies I night need."

"Aunt Agnes, are you still riding?" Mike asked. "I remember when we'd spend hours riding horses around on the ranch, and I loved that. You had several horses back then. What happened to them?"

"After Max died, I got rid of all of them except Missy. I just couldn't part with her. She and I are both getting up there in years, but she seems to be in perfect health. She's twenty-eight now. Every morning I go out to the barn and feed and groom her. Then I exercise her for a while in the paddock. I can't ride her anymore, but I want her to stay in shape. We go back a long way, and I think of her as an old friend. Give me five minutes, and we'll eat. I've already set the table in the dining room. Go on in and sit down. There's some wine on the sideboard. Help yourself."

When they were well into the meal, Mike said, "Aunt Agnes, your cooking is just as good as I remember. That apricot bread was perfect with the lamb. Maybe that's why I decided to marry a woman who owns a restaurant. Kelly, maybe you could get Aunt Agnes to give you that recipe."

Kelly interrupted him, "Agnes, don't believe a word he says. I own a small coffee shop that sits on the end of the municipal pier in Cedar Bay. I'd hardly call it a restaurant, and I would love the recipe for the apricot bread."

"That's not what I hear," Mike said, smiling at Kelly. "Kelly's way too modest. It's common knowledge that people come from miles around to eat at Kelly's Koffee Shop. By the way, I talked to Ralph at the gas station when we first drove into town. He said a lot of wineries have sprung up in the local area, and that people with big bucks are putting money into the town, trying to make it compete with Napa. We went into Lucky Luke's Restaurant when we got here, and I couldn't believe it. Everything's changed from the sawdust on the floor to the menu. We also saw the new bed and breakfast on the edge of town."

"Yes, and that's one reason I wanted you to come for a little visit. You may remember years ago your uncle and I dammed up the stream on our property, so we could have our own water and not have to rely on the city water system. Back then, it wasn't a problem.

John Wilson, the rancher who owns the property just south of here, wasn't very happy about it, but at the time he had plenty of groundwater he could pump. He groused a little about it, but that was about it. However, since the drought here in California has gotten so much worse over the last few years, it's become a problem for him, or so he tells me. He wants to buy the Robertson Ranch, so he can get the water from the stream, or else he wants me to open up the dam. He's offered me a lot of money for the ranch, but I'm not willing to sell it, and I don't want to open up the dam. Your uncle was very clear that we should always have our own independent water supply."

"When did he start approaching you about buying the ranch?" Mike asked.

"A couple of years ago. I told him then I had no intention of selling it. Lately he's become quite angry with me. Then there's some developer who wants me to sell the property to his development corporation. He claims the property would be perfect for a golf course."

"Well, you certainly have enough acreage to do that. What would happen to the house if you sold the ranch?"

"Nothing, because I'm not selling it. Matter of fact I'm working with some other people here in the area to keep this new money that's flowing into the community to a minimum. Can you imagine what would happen to my beautiful ranch if they built a golf course on it? Along with more and more wineries? Calico Gold wouldn't be anything but a name from the past. I wouldn't be surprised if my neighbor John and the developer aren't in cahoots. Maybe he's offered to sell his land to the developer, and he needs mine for the water."

"What can I do to help, Aunt Agnes?" Mike asked in a calm, soothing tone of voice.

"Well, for starters, it can't hurt to let everyone know that my nephew, the sheriff, has come to help his aunt. That might stop the threatening letters I've been getting."

"What are you talking about?" Mike asked, putting his fork down and leaning towards her. "Have you really been getting threatening letters?"

"Yes. Let me get them for you. I'll be back in a minute."

"Mike, I'm really glad we decided to drive down here to see Aunt Agnes. This sounds serious," Kelly said, taking a bite of the apricot bread.

"Yeah, I'm thinking the same thing, but I'm not sure what I can do to help."

Aunt Agnes walked back into the dining room. "Here they are, Mike. I've received three of them. They're postmarked Calico Gold, so they must be from someone around here. They all say the same thing, and the handwriting seems to be the same as well."

Using his pocket knife, so his fingerprints wouldn't be on the letters, Mike carefully unfolded them. He studied each of the letters which contained the words, "It's time for you to leave the ranch."

"Aunt Agnes, I'd consider that a threat. Have you shown these to anyone else?"

"No. I thought about showing them to Chief Robbins, but I was afraid he would think I was just some crazy old lady. Why?"

"If you're the only one who's touched them besides the person who wrote them, we might be able to pick up a fingerprint. It's a long shot, but I think I'll go into town tomorrow and talk to the police chief. Even though the town's small, he probably has some type of a set-up for fingerprinting. Would you get me a couple of plastic bags, and then you can put them in the bags? I don't want to touch them, and your fingerprints are already on them."

When she returned and the threatening letters had been securely placed in the plastic bags, Mike picked up his wine glass and looked into it, seemingly deep in thought. He set it down and turned towards his aunt. "Aunt Agnes, you've always been involved in a lot of things. Why do you think someone sent those letters to you? Are you involved in something I should know about?"

She took a deep breath and said, "I was afraid you were going to ask me that. I told you I only go into town once a week or so, and that's true. What I didn't tell you is that for the last year I've been holding weekly meetings out here at the ranch trying to stop any more development in Calico Gold."

"That doesn't surprise me. Who attends?"

"Well, there's a bunch of people I've known forever who feel just like I do. Matter of fact one of them is in the coming election, running against the judge, Susan Lane, and I'm supporting him. We're pretty sure she's been promising the developer all kinds of things if he'll financially back her election campaign. We have a campaign contribution limit of $2,000 per donor in the county. From what we've found out, she's already gotten $60,000 in campaign contributions. That's a lot of money for a judgeship race, and we've learned that almost all of it came from out of town, even out of state. You may not approve of this, but I've made a vow to myself that Huston Brooks, he's the one running against Judge Lane, will have as much money for this race as Susan Lane does. Believe me, he's going to need it in order for him to beat an incumbent."

"Sounds good on paper, but how do you intend to match that kind of money if there's a donor limit of $2,000 per person? Are you giving people money to give to him?"

"Mike, you're probably better off not knowing some things that I know, but I'm committed to seeing that crooked judge lose her job and having Huston Brooks win, and I'll do whatever it takes."

"So at the moment you have three people who might possibly have written those letters – someone from the corporation who wants to buy the ranch and build a golf course, John Wilson, the rancher who is upset with you because of the water situation, and the judge. Anyone else I should know about?"

Aunt Agnes suddenly took a keen interest in her hands and began to spin her wedding ring around her knobby arthritic ring finger. "Well, now that you mention it, I suppose there are a couple more."

"If I'm going to be able to help you, Aunt Agnes," Mike said gently, "I need to know everything. Please tell me about the other two."

"Remember that shack down by the stream? I've been letting a friend of mine's son live there for a couple of years. He's a Vietnam vet. Something bad happened to him over there, and mentally he's never been the same since he came back from Vietnam. Anyway, he's been doing some strange things lately. I hear screaming coming from the direction of the shack in the middle of the night, and sometimes he comes home really late on his motorcycle and wakes me up when he speeds down the lane. I've heard he's had some problems over at the Roadhouse Bar. Seems to like his liquor a little too much and can't handle it. Guess he gets in a lot of fights. Sometimes I hear a lot of voices coming from the direction of the shack, and I'm pretty sure he's been bringing people back to the ranch after the Roadhouse closes. Anyway, I don't like it. I asked him to stop, but he hasn't. I'm beginning to feel unsafe here in my own home because of him."

She swallowed several times. "A week ago I told him he'd have to find another place to live. I told him I needed to have someone live in that shack who was a little more dependable."

"How did he take it?"

"Not well. I took Sam with me, because I thought I might need a little protection. We went over to the shack, and I told him. He was so angry he slammed his fist into one of the walls of the shack and made a hole in it. I'm afraid of him, and I'm not used to feeling like that."

"I don't blame you. I'll go over there and talk to him. Maybe when he sees that I'm here, he'll leave. You want to tell me about the other person?"

"Not really, but I guess I'm going to have to sooner or later."

"Aunt Agnes, please tell me."

"All right. Did your mother ever tell you she had a sister other than me?"

"Are you kidding? No, she always said she had one sister, that would be you, and no brothers, and that her family was a two child family long before it became fashionable to have only two children."

"Well, we did have a sister. Her name was Rachel. Sixty years ago if a woman got pregnant, she was an outcast. Remember the book called The Scarlet Letter and Hester Prynne, the young woman in the book who was required to wear a scarlet letter 'A' on her dress which stood for adulteress? Well, it wasn't a lot better for our sister. God bless our parents, but they were very conservative people, and they made Rachel leave and go stay with one of dad's relatives to have the baby. After she had the baby, she never came back. Our parents made your mother and me promise we would never have anything to do with her. They said she had shamed the family and just like Hester in The Scarlet Letter book, whenever they thought of her, in their minds she was wearing a scarlet letter."

"Do you know whatever happened to her?"

"Yes, I'm getting to that. I may have promised my parents I wouldn't have anything to do with her, but after they died, I got in touch with Rachel, and I'm glad I did. She had cancer and was near the end. I went to see her, and she died a short time later." She paused and wiped a small tear from her eye.

"Why do I get the feeling there's more to this?" Mike asked.

"Because there is. Rachel had a son out of wedlock. She raised him and scraped and saved to send him to college. He's an artist, and like you always hear, he's a struggling artist. She made me promise I would watch over him after she was gone. I didn't have a choice, so I promised. He lives in the hills about ten miles from here. His name is Daniel Noonan."

"Wait a minute. That was yours and mom's maiden name. So she never even gave Daniel his father's name?"

"Mike, here's the thing. Rachel had what was known at that time as 'round heels.' Today people would have probably called her 'promiscuous'. I'm not sure she even knew who the baby's father was. Anyway, I bought a small cabin up in the hills for Daniel. He's a real loner. I think he may feel like a freak, because he walks with a very bad limp. Evidently he was playing in the street when he was a child and a car hit him and injured his leg. He comes here for dinner on a regular basis. You hate to say this about your own nephew, but he's a real loser.

"His mother took care of him until she died, and I've taken care of him pretty much ever since. He made a comment when he was here at dinner the other night. He told me when he inherited the Robertson Ranch, he was really looking forward to living in the Robertson House. That's when I did a stupid thing. I told him he wouldn't be inheriting the house or the ranch, and that I had named my nephew, Mike Reynolds, as the sole beneficiary under the terms of my Will. Mike, I've decided I want you to have everything. I know the Robertson House and the ranch will be in good hands under your ownership."

"You what? Aunt Agnes, I never expected you to do something like that. Why don't you give the ranch to one of the causes you've worked so hard for over the years? I don't need it, although I'm really touched you think enough of me that you'd leave it to me. What was his reaction?" Mike asked as he sat back in his chair, clearly shocked.

"He was furious. He called me a bunch of names and said I owed it to him for what my family had done to his mother. I told him I didn't owe him a dime, and it was about time he became a man and took care of himself. He jumped up from the dining room table, stormed out the front door, slammed it behind him, and left. That was the last time I saw him. I haven't heard from him since."

"Aunt Agnes, I'm so glad you called and asked me to come down here. I need to think about this and figure out what we can do to make sure you're safe. I remember as a kid you were a crack shot. Do you still have a gun?"

"Sure do, and I'm still a crack shot, if I don't say so myself."

"Keep it near you. Can't hurt. And keep your dog, Sam, with you. Kelly's had a few experiences lately when a gun and a dog have come in real handy. We'll clear the table for you and do the dishes. You did enough for us by preparing this great meal. I think you should get some sleep, and we'll talk in the morning. I need to think a little more about this whole situation."

She stood up and lightly touched him on the cheek. "Thanks for coming. I already feel better knowing you're here. See you in the morning."

Mike would never forget what she looked like as she walked away from the table and the feel of her warm soft hand on his cheek. It was the last time he would see her alive.

CHAPTER TWELVE

Mike got out of bed early the next morning and said, "Kelly, stay where you are. I'll make some coffee and bring it up after I let the dogs out. Rebel's been whining for the last half hour. Think he misses his own home. Don't know about you, but I could get used to sleeping in a four poster bed. Felt like I was floating on a white puffy cloud. Did you sleep okay?"

"Absolutely great. What do you have in mind for today?"

"Coffee and breakfast, in that order. Think I'll go into town and visit the police chief. I want to introduce myself to him, and I'd like to know if he can pick up any fingerprints from those letters."

"Those letters worry me, Mike. Sounds like there are a number of people who could have sent them. I thought I might go into town and see what I can find out. There's always some place that's the local gossip center. Usually it's a restaurant, but from the looks of the one we saw yesterday, it was a little too upscale to cater to the locals."

"Okay. Plan on going into town with me, but right now this man needs coffee. I'll be back in a few minutes with a cup for you."

*****

"That was fast," Kelly said as Mike pushed the bedroom door open with his hip, a cup of steaming coffee in each hand. "Thanks. How's Aunt Agnes this morning?"

"Don't know. She wasn't in the kitchen. She mentioned last night that she goes out to the barn and exercises Missy every morning. When I finish this coffee, I'll go see if I can give her a hand."

"Rather imagine she has her own way of doing things from what I've seen of her. You might just get in the way," Kelly said laughing.

"You're probably right. She's an opinionated strong-willed woman, and like Ralph at the gas station said, kind of a living legend in this town. No one wants to cross her, and everyone's afraid of her."

"That may be so, but from what she told us last night, it sounds like there are a few people who aren't afraid to cross her."

After he finished his coffee, Mike showered and got dressed, "Back in a few. I'm going out to the barn. Lady, Rebel, come."

Kelly finished dressing and walked downstairs to get another cup of coffee. She expected Mike to be seated at the table, reading the paper, as he usually did each morning. There was no sign of him, and she heard Rebel whimpering. The sound came from the direction of the barn. She walked outside and headed towards it. As she approached the barn, she thought she heard someone crying. She hurried to the door and quickly took in the scene in front of her. Mike was holding Aunt Agnes' hand, crying, while Lady, Rebel, and Sam stood next to him, softly whining. She ran over to Mike.

"What's happened? Did she fall? Is she alive? Should I call an ambulance?"

"No, she's dead," Mike said between sobs. "She's been murdered. Someone struck her on the back of the head. I'll never forgive myself for letting her come out here by herself after those threats."

"Mike, you can't blame yourself. She's been coming out here every morning, probably for as long as she's lived on the ranch. You had no way of knowing that someone really meant to do her harm. You stay here, and I'll go in the house and call the police."

She ran to the house and in a shaking voice made the call. A few minutes later she heard the sound of police sirens, and two police cars raced up the lane and pulled to a stop in front of the house. She opened the door and waved them in.

"You must be the wife of Agnes' nephew. She was always talking about him, and she couldn't wait to meet you. I'm Police Chief Robbins. Where is she?"

"In the barn. Mike's with her," she said, tears gathering in her eyes. "He thinks someone hit her on the back of the head and killed her. This is not going to be easy for him. Even though he didn't see her very often, they spoke on the phone almost weekly."

"Murder's never easy for any relative, and unfortunately Agnes had her share of enemies. I'm sure there are a number of people who'd like to see her dead. I called the county coroner. He should be here in a few minutes."

Kelly and Mike spent the rest of morning talking to the police, the coroner, and the people who began to come to the ranch as soon as they heard the news. The police chief and his deputy searched the area for clues, particularly in and around the barn. They had no luck finding the weapon that had been used to murder Aunt Agnes.

Mike walked over to Kelly and said, "Could you talk to the people who are starting to show up at the front door? Just tell them we have no idea what happened other than the fact that she was murdered. I really need to talk to Chief Robbins without anyone around."

"Of course. Take your time. I'm just not sure there's enough room in the refrigerator for all this food everyone's bringing."

"There used to be another one in the garage. I haven't been out there since we got here. Check it out. I'll be back in a few minutes."

He and Chief Robbins went into the study which Aunt Agnes had used as an office, and Mike closed the door behind them.

CHAPTER THIRTEEN

"Please have a seat, Chief Robbins. There are some things I think you need to know that my aunt told me last night. They may have a bearing on her murder."

"First of all," the chief said, "let me tell you how sorry I am about the loss of your aunt. Agnes was one of my heroes. She never turned away from something difficult, and I can't imagine what this town would be like if she hadn't been so active in trying to keep out the big city money. A few of them were able to get in, but without her leadership, the town we know today as Calico Gold wouldn't be here. The personality of the town would be gone, and it would be just another tourist trap in California's gold country. She was a remarkable woman, and I'm going to miss her. She spoke of you often and said that although you didn't see each other too much, she regarded you as her son. Rest assured I'll do everything in my power to find the person who murdered your aunt. Agnes told me you're a county sheriff up in Oregon, so any assistance you can give me in finding the killer would be a big help."

"Thanks, Chief, I appreciate it. I've decided to stay here for a few days and see what I can do about finding the killer. You can deputize me or just use me however you want, but for now, there's something I want to show you."

He walked over to the desk and took out the letters he had put there after he and Kelly had finished cleaning up the night before. "At dinner last night my aunt told me she had received these letters during the past week. There's no doubt in my mind they represent a threat to her. I was going to go to the police station today and see if you have a fingerprint machine or something that might be able to pick up any prints on them other than my aunt's."

Chief Robbins spent several minutes looking at the letters. "I agree, Mike. These are definitely threatening. Yes, we do have a machine, and I'll see what I can pick up. Tell me about the conversation you had with your aunt."

Mike related what his aunt had told him last night about the people who possibly could have sent the letters to her. "Chief, it seems like quite a coincidence that my aunt would receive three threatening letters, and then she's murdered. I don't believe in coincidences. I think there's a very good chance that the person who sent her those letters is the person who murdered her. Would you agree?"

"In theory, yes. If we could find out who wrote the letters, I believe that would be enough evidence to warrant an arrest, but it doesn't mean that's the person who killed her. In other words, we'd need more evidence than a match between fingerprints. What are you thinking?"

"Once we establish a match, we'd have to find out where that person was at the time of the murder. Of course, there's always the chance that it was a hired killer, particularly if it was the developer. I can't see him getting his hands dirty by becoming directly involved in a homicide. My aunt was rather vague on the developer's identity, but Ralph at the gas station might know something."

"I don't think you have to even bother with Ralph. The developer's from San Francisco, and his name is Richard Martin. He specializes in building resorts and golf courses. I always like to know who's planning on doing what in this town in order to keep one step ahead of trouble. Anyway, city hall employees tell me when they get wind that someone is interested in building in Calico Gold.

"This guy has been trying to get a foothold in this area for five years and has been getting much more aggressive of late. You have to admit that the Robertson Ranch would make a spectacular golf course with its hills, the stream, the lake, and the hundreds of old oak trees. He was also nosing around trying to find out if the Robertson House was on some Historical Home Registry. He mentioned that if and when your aunt sold it to him, he was going to modernize the house and make it into a boutique hotel."

"No wonder my aunt was fighting so hard. To see this house made into a hotel would have killed her."

"Well, it might very well have been the reason she was murdered. On a related subject, Mike, I have to ask you something. You told me you were shocked when your aunt told you last night she was going to leave the ranch and the house to you in her Will. Was last night the first time she had ever discussed it with you?"

"Yes. I had no idea she intended to do that. And I know what you're thinking. It would be the same thing I would think if I were in your shoes. Who has the most to gain when someone is murdered? In this case, it would probably be me, but I did not murder my aunt. Number one, I had no idea she was going to will everything to me. Number two, she asked me to come here, and even Ralph mentioned she'd told him that she'd asked me to come, and number three, those letters were postmarked as having been mailed from Calico Gold. I didn't get here until late yesterday, and I have a number of people who will vouch that I was in Cedar Bay until yesterday morning."

"Mike, I believe you, but let me ask you this. Do you have an alibi for the time of the murder?"

"I was with Kelly and the dogs here in the house. Kelly can vouch I was with her until I went to the barn and found my aunt."

"You're a lawman. You know it's not uncommon for a married person to lie in order to protect their spouse. If your cousin is angry that you're going to inherit the ranch, he may try and get back at you by saying that she's covering for you. Better be prepared for that."

"I've never met him, but I sure don't like what I'm hearing. Do you know him?"

"There's not much that goes on in Calico Gold I don't know about. He's not a very friendly sort, kind of a hermit. He's never been in trouble with the law, but there's nothing likable about the guy. Heard through the rumor mill a while ago he was your aunt's nephew, and that she was taking care of him financially. I've seen a couple of his paintings in town. Not my style. They're dark and kind of scary. I don't think he sells very many, but Cindy, the woman who owns the gallery where they're displayed, likes to showcase local artists. She told me once tourists like to buy a painting that's from a local artist when they visit a town."

"All right. I'm prepared to be considered a suspect until I can clear my name, but let me worry about that. I would think you could get a sample of handwriting from the judge in the form of something she's signed. We could have an expert compare the handwriting sample with the writing on the letters and see if there's a match. I can probably get something from Gary when I talk to him. As small as Calico Gold is, I wouldn't think you'd have a handwriting expert here."

"No. If we pick up anything, I'll send it to the Department of Justice in Sacramento. I've got a friend there who analyzes handwriting. They help small towns out with things like that, and it won't be a problem."

He was interrupted by a knock on the door. He opened it and saw that it was Kelly.

"I'm sorry to interrupt, but the minister is here to discuss tomorrow's service. I told him you'd be with him shortly."

"Thanks, sweetheart." Mike turned towards Chief Robbins, "I think that's about it for now. I need to make arrangements for the funeral tomorrow. It's going to be at 2:00 in the afternoon. I'll stop by your office afterwards if I've found out anything."

"Mike, I'll be at the funeral. Your aunt was a great lady, and I want to honor her, as will probably most of the people in town."

CHAPTER FOURTEEN

Thirty minutes later, Mike said, "Thank you for coming, Reverend," as he walked with him towards the door. "We'll see you tomorrow, and please tell the women at the church I really appreciate their offer to help with the food here at the house after the funeral."

"Not a problem. Your aunt was pretty special to a lot of people. Oh, by the way, my secretary and another church helper will be coming to the house momentarily to see what they can do to help."

"Again, thanks for everything," Mike said as he closed the door and turned to Kelly.

"Mike, I know it sounds impossible, but maybe you should go upstairs and see if you can get some sleep. The next few days are going to be pretty hectic. By the way, I called Julia and told her about Agnes. Being the good daughter she is, she immediately called me back after she'd talked to Brad, and the two of them, along with the girls, are coming here for a few days to help in any way they can. Couldn't ask for a better daughter or son-in-law. They're driving over from San Francisco and will be here late tonight. The phone has been ringing off the hook, and I could use some help, so I'm really glad they're coming. Between the phone and the people coming to the door bringing food, I'm getting overwhelmed."

"I had a phone call from my aunt's attorney. He's coming over in a few minutes. He wants to talk to me about her Will. You want to sit in on the conversation?"

"I'm going to pass. We left Cedar Bay so quickly I had to cancel my bi-monthly appointment to have my hair trimmed. I really want to get it done before the funeral. It's looking pretty scraggly, and I'll catch the devil from Julia if I don't. You know how Julia is when it comes to you. She's fiercely protective of anything to do with you since you gave her away at her wedding and also gave the toast that brought tears to everyone's eyes. She'll tell me I have to represent you, and that people will really be scrutinizing me. She's probably right. I thought I'd go into town. I saw a beauty shop when we drove in yesterday, and I noticed they had a sign that said they took walk-ins."

"Okay. I can hold the fort down here. Where are the dogs?"

"Lady and Rebel have befriended Sam. Poor guy, he's been going from room to room looking for your aunt, but a few minutes ago, I noticed that all three of them were asleep. It's a good thing we brought Lady and Rebel. Sam needs a little company."

"Not only for Sam, but for us as well. Don't forget there's a killer on the loose, and he's been on this property. That's why I'm glad we have the dogs with us. You promised me that you'll always carry that gun I gave you. Still have it in your purse?"

"Yes. I'm never without it, but I don't think I'd be the target here. If anyone is a potential target, I think it would be you. You've replaced your aunt as the owner of the ranch, so someone might be after you as well."

"I'm well aware of that. I've got my gun, and you know what a great guard dog Rebel is, so I'm sure we'll be fine."

"So am I, but I really wonder what's going to happen to the Robertson Ranch now. Be willing to bet you're going to be contacted by at least a couple of people today or right after the funeral who want to buy it."

"I'm sure you're right. Kelly, have you thought about what we're going to do with the ranch? I'm having a hard time dealing with all of this. It's totally unexpected. We can't pick up and leave Cedar Bay and live here, but on the other hand I don't want to sell the ranch and see a golf course built on it."

"Want my advice, sheriff? Sit on it for a few days. Too much has happened, and you might regret any decision you make now. There's no hurry. Julia said they could stay a couple of weeks, and I'm sure I can as well. Plus you could probably get some time off from the Sheriff's Department for bereavement leave. Let's see what the next few days bring. Gotta go, the doorbell's ringing."

She returned a few minutes later. "Mike, this is Jim Warren, your aunt's attorney, and the two women from the church have arrived. They're going to take care of the phone and door while I'm gone. I'll be back in an hour or two. I just let the dogs out, so they should be fine while I'm gone." She pulled the door shut behind her as she headed outside towards their car.

*****

"It's nice to meet you, Jim. Thanks for coming out here," Mike said to the silver haired lawyer who wore an open collar shirt with freshly pressed jeans and expensive looking cowboy boots. "I'm usually on the other side of situations like this, the lawman side, so dealing with the aftermath of a murder from a family perspective is quite new to me." He shook Jim's hand. "Please, have a seat. What can I do for you?"

"I don't think there's anything you can do for me but listen." He opened the worn brown leather briefcase he'd been carrying and took out a file. "Your aunt made a Will a few years ago. It specifically names you as the sole beneficiary of the Robertson Ranch and everything else that was your aunt's." He looked over the top of his bifocals at Mike. "Everything else would include Sam, Missy, the barn, and all of her investments, which were not insignificant. I can give you the exact amount as of the date of death in a day or so. The Will also specifically says that no other relative is to inherit any part of the ranch property." He looked up from the Will he was reading.

"I'm not a lawyer," Mike said, "but that sounds to me like she did not want her other nephew, who I just found out about last night, to inherit anything. Would that be right?"

"You're absolutely correct. She told me about her nephew, Daniel Noonan, several years ago. She didn't like him but felt she owed something to him for the way her family had treated his mother. She also told me she'd made a deathbed promise to her sister to watch over him. Agnes mentioned he came to dinner occasionally, but that he'd never made an attempt to be a real nephew to her. Reading between the lines, I gathered he hadn't offered to help her in any way as she was getting older. I'm sure she could have used some help.

"She's been his sole support, and we talked about what would happen to him when she was gone. I agreed with her that if he didn't inherit anything from her, maybe he'd be forced to do something on his own. Although she was a very strong woman in many ways, she had a weak spot when it came to him and his mother. She couldn't bring herself to stop giving him an allowance, which I'd been advising her to do for quite a while.

"Agnes spoke very highly of you. I don't know if you're aware of it, but there is also a provision in the Will for the financial maintenance of the ranch. She loved the Robertson House and this ranch. She told me several people were trying to get her to sell it, but she had no intention of doing so."

"That's pretty much what she told me last night," Mike said. "I've never even met this cousin. It certainly says something about his character given the fact he wanted this house and the property, but he never tried to help my aunt out. I suppose I'll meet him some day, maybe even at the funeral, but I'm pretty sure I'm not going to like him."

"I've met him a couple of times, and I would have to agree with you. I don't think you're going to like him."

"Well, counselor, what's next?"

"I'm going to court this afternoon and file the necessary paperwork to have you named as the interim person who has the power to sign checks and anything that's necessary to keep the ranch running until everything is legally transferred over to you. Here are a couple of papers I need you to sign," he said, handing a pen and the papers to Mike. "Just write your name where the red "X" marks appear. That's all I need from you. Once they're filed, I'll have Judge Lane sign off on them, and you'll be good to go."

"Jim, I assume anything I tell you is privileged information since you're an attorney, and I believe now we have an attorney-client relationship. Would I be correct?"

"Yes," he said quizzically. "Why do you ask?"

"Aunt Agnes told me she was supporting a young man who was running against Judge Lane in the upcoming election. Would it be better to get another judge to sign off on these papers?"

"No. We're in a pretty remote area here in Calico Gold, and she's the only judge around these parts. If it will make you feel any better, I'm sure she'll be happy to sign off on them. If the rumors are true, that out of town developers are funding her re-election campaign, the judge and her supporters should be happy there's a chance the property will be sold now that Agnes is deceased."

"In a twisted way, you're probably right," Mike said, standing up. "Again, Jim, thanks for coming out here. You certainly saved me a trip to town, and with everything that needs doing and the decisions that need to be made, I'm kind of tight on time."

"No problem. Happy to do it for Agnes. I'll call you and let you know when the judge signs off on the paperwork. If there's anything you need from me, or if you have any questions, feel free to call me. Here's my card. See you at the funeral."

CHAPTER FIFTEEN

Kelly felt like she'd taken a step back in time when she walked into Betty's Salon. The walls were covered with posters of lipsticks, products for permanents, and makeup ads. Kelly remembered the names from when she was a child. There was even one for Johnson's Baby Oil – "Cover Yourself in Baby Oil and Get the Tan of Your Life."

Right, Kelly thought. *I wonder how many people are paying for that today with wrinkled skin. Glad it was usually overcast, cloudy, and rainy where I grew up. Who knows what I'd look like if I'd gotten a lot of sun?*

"May I help you?" asked the young receptionist, never taking her eyes away from her cell phone.

"Yes. I don't have an appointment, but I'd like to get my hair trimmed."

The young woman reluctantly looked away from her phone and examined the appointment book in front of her.

Of course there would be an appointment book and not a computer. I'll bet nothing has changed in here since this place opened. They even have the old chair style hair dryers I remember from Wanda's Salon when my mother took me there as a kid.

There were two hairdressers working and they, too, looked like they'd been stuck in time. They had identical large backcombed beehive hairdos which probably looked great in the 60's, but not so much now.

The receptionist walked over to one of them who looked at Kelly and said, "Have a seat. I'll be through here in a few minutes, and I can take you then."

While she waited, Kelly leafed through some of the beauty magazines that were scattered on a nearby table. She wondered if the hairdressers would be able to duplicate any of the hair styles in them if a customer asked. She doubted it.

"Honey, come on over here. I'm Betty, and I'm ready for you," the large hairdresser with the pancake makeup and bright red lipstick said. Her lipstick was a shade lighter than her hair color. She wore light blue eye shadow, and her eyes were accented by a heavy band of black eyeliner. It was hard for Kelly not to simply stare, and she was very glad she only needed a trim and nothing more. It was obvious there was a vast difference in their taste in makeup.

"What do you need today?"

"I need a trim. Not a cut, just about ½" taken off," Kelly said.

"Piece of cake, honey. Don't think I've seen you around here before. New to Calico Gold?"

"Yes and no. I've never been here before, but my husband was here a lot when he was younger."

"Well, welcome to Calico Gold. What's your husband's name?"

"I don't think you'd recognize it, but I'm sure you knew his aunt, Agnes Johnson."

Betty's scissors came to an abrupt stop, and the room became quiet. Everyone's eyes in the little shop were focused on Kelly.

"Knew Agnes well. I hear she was murdered this morning, and her funeral's gonna be tomorrow. Is that true?"

"Yes, unfortunately it is," Kelly said as tears welled up in her eyes. "I'm sorry, it was just such a shock."

"You don't need to apologize. I imagine it was. Do they know who did it?"

"No, but the police chief is working on it. I guess Agnes had some enemies."

"You can say that again, but she also had a lot of friends. Town's practically split apart over whether it should become a destination tourist trap or continue like it's always been. There's real strong feelings on both sides. I happen to agree with your husband's aunt. I like Calico Gold just the way it is."

She was interrupted by an attractive older woman who had just finished having her hair cut by the other beautician. She wore an expensive knit suit which had a very short skirt, cheapening the overall effect. Her hair was dyed blond, and she wore bright red nail polish on her fingers and toes which could be seen through her peek-a-boo high-heeled sandals. She was heavily made up.

"I'm sorry to interrupt you, but I couldn't help but overhear your conversation. I'm Judge Susan Lane. Your husband's aunt and I were certainly on different sides of the fence regarding the future development of Calico Gold, but I'm sorry to hear she died and even sorrier to hear she was murdered."

Wow! This must be the judge Aunt Agnes mentioned last night.

"Thank you. I only met her yesterday, but I really liked her, and obviously, my husband is quite broken up. She was his only relative, and they were quite close."

"Please give him my condolences. I'll be attending the funeral tomorrow. What's going to happen to Agnes' ranch? I understand several people would like to buy the Robertson Ranch."

"Under the terms of Agnes' Will, the ranch and all of her estate will go to my husband, but he hasn't made any decisions regarding the ranch. There are too many other things that need attending to first. Agnes told us at dinner last night she didn't want her property developed. I don't know if that will affect his decision, but I suspect it will."

"You never know. People say one thing, and then when they see how much money they can make by ignoring what the deceased person wanted, they tend to forget about it. Money can be very seductive."

"You don't know my husband. Money has never been that important to him."

"Sorry to disagree with you, but it's been my experience that money can and often is more important than anything else. It's been nice talking to you. I have to hear some cases this afternoon. See you tomorrow at the funeral."

That is not a nice person. No wonder Agnes was funding the young man's campaign who's running against her. Think I'll make a contribution to him as well.

"Honey, don't pay no attention to the judge," Betty said. "She don't know when to keep her mouth shut sometimes. They say she's a good judge, but I sure have my doubts. Lots of rumors about her being in the pocket of the big real estate developers. Might be some truth to that. They say if you do what she says and one of your family's in trouble, the judge is real lenient, but if you go against her and one of yours is unfortunate enough to have some legal problem, it's gonna be a bigger problem by the time she's through with you. Don't know. Just sayin' what I hear, and you can't begin to imagine everything I hear in this shop."

"I'm not surprised. I own a coffee shop in a small town in

Oregon, and everyone comes there to gossip. It's probably the same here."

"It is. I heard about Agnes' death about the same time the police chief got to the Robertson Ranch this morning. It was all over town in minutes. Even heard when and where the funeral's gonna be held. Everyone's talking about what's gonna happen to the ranch. A lot of people want the money that would come from increased tourism if a golf course was built on the property, and a lot of people don't want the tourism and don't want the ranch sold to some out-of-town developer. Guess is, your husband's probably going to be pressured from both sides in the next few days. Kinda feel sorry for him, although it's hard to feel sorry for anyone who's suddenly that rich."

"I'm sorry, I don't understand what you mean," Kelly said.

"Well, everyone knows Agnes was a very rich woman. Her lawyer's secretary gets her hair done here, and she told me Agnes was probably the richest person in Calico Gold. Figure she'd know if anyone would. Heck, in a town this small everyone knows everyone else's business. Not much else to do. Hear she had a lot of stocks and investments and was a multimillionaire in her own right. Since your husband's the sole beneficiary of Agnes' Will, that means he's gonna get everything. That'll make him a millionaire, just like Agnes was."

"I have no idea what his inheritance might amount to, and I don't think he does either."

"Well, the townspeople sure think he's gonna get a bundle." She finished trimming Kelly's hair and handed her a mirror so she could look at the back of her head.

"Looks great, Betty, thanks."

"You can pay the receptionist on your way out. It was nice to meet you. Tell your husband I'm sorry about his aunt. Might want to tell him to be real careful. I'm thinkin' if Agnes was murdered, someone maybe wanted somethin' from her, and now that she's gone, your husband just might have what the killer wanted."

"Thank you. I'll tell him."

Like he doesn't already know.

CHAPTER SIXTEEN

Kelly had just pressed the automatic car door lock on her car after leaving Betty's Salon when a woman said, "Kelly, please wait," in a loud voice. Kelly turned around and saw a woman walking quickly towards her dressed in a T-shirt, sweat pants, and expensive looking tennis shoes.

"Thanks. I'm Lucy Thomas, a friend of your husband's aunt. I was in Betty's Salon and couldn't help but overhear your conversation. A friend of mine called me early this morning to tell me about Agnes' death. I can't believe it. Even though she was quite a bit older than me, we became very good friends. In fact, I often ate dinner at the Robertson House. If you have a minute, I'd like to talk to you."

"It's nice to meet you, Lucy. Why don't we get in my car and talk there, rather than standing here on the sidewalk?"

"Thanks. My feet would appreciate it. I love to walk and often walk more than ten miles a day, but at times my feet let me know they're maxed out."

After they got in the car she said, "I'd like to tell you a little story. I'm one of the people who has been going to Agnes' home for the weekly meetings she held trying to keep future development out of Calico Gold." The attractive fortyish woman reached in the small purse she had clipped to her belt and pulled out a tissue. She wiped her eyes and said, "I'm sorry. I'm having a very hard time dealing with her death. She saved my life."

"What do you mean?" Kelly asked.

"Let me start again. After I heard the terrible news about Agnes, it seems like my mind hasn't been working as well as it should be. I just can't get the mental picture of Agnes being murdered out of my mind." She briefly paused and then resumed, "Seven months ago my husband left me for a younger woman. I thought we had the perfect marriage. He had a good job, and I've been a teacher for twenty years, so money wasn't an issue. He just fell out of love with me." Her voice broke, and she looked out the window for a few moments trying to regain her composure.

"As you can see, I'm still devastated by it. It came out of the blue. I know it sounds ridiculous, but I didn't have a clue he was unhappy. If anyone had asked, I would have said we were as close as any married couple could be. I was wrong. After he left me, it was all I could do to get to school and teach. I was angry and suffered from severe depression. I didn't have anything to live for. I stopped attending the weekly meetings at Agnes'. One afternoon just after I'd gotten home from school, she called me and asked if she could come over. She and Sam, that big collie of hers, came to the house, and she talked to me for over an hour."

"What a kind thing for her to do," Kelly said.

"It was more than kind. As I mentioned before, she literally saved my life. She saw how angry I was and made a suggestion that I took to heart. She told me I had to find an outlet for my anger, or it would consume me. She suggested I start walking. Quite honestly, I was a little overweight then. I've often wondered if that was one of the reasons my husband left me."

"You're certainly not overweight now," Kelly said, looking at the trim athletic figure of the woman sitting next to her.

"Thanks, but you wouldn't have said that if you'd seen me then. Anyway, I started walking, and I became addicted to walking. I was literally walking off my anger. I started getting up an hour earlier than usual, and I'd walk for an hour and then go to school. During my lunch break at school I walked. For an hour in the late afternoon I walked. The weight came off, and I could feel the anger and depression lifting. It was all because of Agnes. After she came to my home that day, she invited me over for dinner quite often, and we became very good friends."

"I'm sorry I'm not going to have the chance to really get to know her," Kelly said. "I met her last night for the first time and thought she was one of the most interesting people I'd ever met."

"She was. I wanted to give you the background of my relationship with Agnes before I told you what I'm about to tell you. I don't know if Agnes had a chance to tell you about the letters she'd been getting in the mail. She was concerned and thought they could have come from one of several people."

"Yes, she told us about them last night."

"As soon as I heard she'd been murdered I thought there had to be a connection between the letters and her death. There were five people she suspected might have sent them to her. One was Judge Lane. She's running for re-election, and Agnes was financially backing her opponent, Huston Brooks. Judge Lane is very close to a developer in San Francisco. I've seen him over at her house on my walks. He drives a silver Lexus."

"Have you actually seen him? He seems to be somewhat of a mystery man. Agnes said she had never met him."

"Yes. I've seen the back of his head when he was going into Judge Lane's house. That's all. Agnes also thought there might have been some type of relationship between the developer and a rancher by the name of John Wilson. He owns the ranch that adjoins the Robertson Ranch and from what Agnes told me, he was desperate to get water for his ranch. He kept asking her to open up the dam on her ranch or else sell him her ranch."

"That's three of the people. She told us there were two others. Did you know them?"

"Several times when I was at the ranch for dinner, her nephew, Daniel Noonan, joined us. I didn't care for him, and I don't think Agnes did either. There certainly didn't seem to be any genuine warmth between them. Several months ago she told me she had made your husband the sole beneficiary of her Will. I remember asking her how she thought her other nephew, Daniel, would take that news."

"What did she say?" Kelly asked.

"She said she didn't think he was going to take it well. In fact, a few days ago she mentioned she was going to tell him when he came to dinner the next night. Also, there was one other person she was concerned about, the guy who lives in the little shack down by the stream that runs through the ranch."

"I've heard he's got a temper. Agnes said she asked him to move out of the shack, and he got very angry. Do you know anything about that?"

"No more than what you just said. I met him once, and I sure didn't think she needed someone like that living on her property. If he's left the ranch, I haven't heard about it.

"I know I've done a lot of talking, and I really thank you for listening to me, but here's one more thing that might be of interest to you. As I mentioned, I like to walk a lot. Usually I walk early in the morning, around 5:00 a.m. That way I can finish my walk, take a shower, and be at school by 7:30 a.m. I try to vary my route so I won't get bored, and I often walk out to the Robertson Ranch, and I even walk around on the property itself. It was fine with Agnes if I did that. As a matter of fact, she was the one who suggested it.

"The day before yesterday, I was walking out by the ranch when a silver Lexus drove down the lane from Agnes' ranch and turned onto the highway. It was barely light, but I clearly saw that the passenger in the car was Judge Lane. The developer she's been seeing for quite a few months drives a silver Lexus. I remember thinking at the time that it was strange they'd be visiting the ranch that early in the morning. I made a mental note to ask Agnes about it the next time I saw her." She put her head in her hands and cried softly. "I never saw her again. I keep thinking about why the two of them would be driving around out by Agnes' ranch at that time of day and wonder if it had something to do with her murder."

"I agree. It seems really odd. I'll tell my husband about it. He's working with Chief Robbins trying to help solve the murder. Maybe it does have something to do with Agnes' death. I know this has been hard for you, Lucy, and I really want to thank you. I'm sure I'll see you at the funeral tomorrow, and I hope you'll come to the house afterwards."

"When she was alive, I did whatever I could for Agnes, and tomorrow if she's looking down from heaven to see who's attending her funeral, I want to make sure she sees me."

"I'm sure she will," Kelly said.

"Oh, I almost forgot to mention something else that's been bothering me. Everyone knew that Agnes went out to the barn first thing in the morning to groom and feed Missy. If someone was intent on killing her that would be the easiest place to do it."

"If everyone knew, you're probably right."

Lucy opened the door and turned back to Kelly. "Please do me a favor, and let your husband know his aunt saved my life. I don't think I'd be here today if it weren't for her."

"I certainly will. Again, thanks for telling me all of this. Hopefully, we can make some use out of it. See you tomorrow."

CHAPTER SEVENTEEN

Early that evening, after the last person had expressed their condolences and left, Mike closed the door and took a deep breath. "Kelly, I don't know when I've been so tired, and we still have tomorrow to get through. I hope I can make it. I feel like I'm putting my feelings on hold, and I know that's not healthy. What I'd really like to do is just get in bed and go to sleep. Real macho man, I am, huh?"

"Mike, this has to be one of the worst days of your life. If you want to go to bed and sleep, I'll understand, but if not, why don't you sit down, and I'll get you a glass of wine. You can talk to me while I make dinner. I saw some jumbo pasta shells in the pantry that I can stuff. I'll mix some of the different cheeses your aunt had in the refrigerator with some Italian sausage and some Italian herbs. A little marinara sauce, and I'll be good to go. Your aunt has all the necessary ingredients, so it will be easy. Actually, I'll be creating a new recipe. If it turns out the way I hope it will, the dish will probably show up on the menu at Kelly's Koffee Shop."

"That sounds wonderful. Kind of a cross between lasagna and manicotti. I'm all in."

"Here's your wine. I have a feeling something else is bothering you besides the death of your aunt. What's the matter?"

He twirled the glass of wine in his hand for a long time and then slowly began to speak, "Kelly, you've been involved in solving other murder cases with me, and you know I've always told you to start with who has the most to gain when a person is murdered. Well, guess what? I have the most to gain by Aunt Agnes' death, so that makes me a suspect. If it was my case, I'd probably put me at the top of the list. I'm really frustrated because I don't know how I'm going to prove my innocence."

"Mike I was with you until you found your aunt in the barn. You can't be serious. Who would possibly think you did it?"

"Well for one, the police chief. Oh, he was nice enough about it, but I'm sure he has his doubts. If I were him, I would too."

"Do you know the approximate time she was murdered?"

"No. That will be in the coroner's report, and we'll probably get it tomorrow or the next day. Why?"

"You were asleep in bed with me until you went downstairs to make coffee. You wouldn't have had time to go out to the barn and murder your aunt. It couldn't have happened during the night, because she was dressed in different clothes than what she was wearing the night before. It had to have happened early this morning."

"That's true, but people lie all the time to protect their spouses. I'm sure that's what everyone would think if you provide an alibi for me."

"I know you didn't do it. I'll just have to find out who did, so your name will be cleared."

"Kelly, we've had this conversation too many times to repeat it. I don't want you involved in trying to solve this case. I'll find out who did it, not you. Would you promise me you won't get involved?"

"Of course," she said, mentally crossing her fingers behind her back. "However, I do have some thoughts I'd like to share with you."

"Somehow, I was sure you would. Shoot, and could you get me another glass of wine?"

"Here you be," she said as she refilled his wine glass with a fresh crisp Chardonnay. "This is what I'm thinking. Your aunt told us about five people who she thought could have possibly sent those letters to her. I think all five of them would qualify as suspects. We just have to figure out which one did it."

"That sounds a bit simplistic, sweetheart, don't you think?"

"Let me finish. The letters were all handwritten. I think our best chance for solving this is to find out who wrote the letters. If it's any one of the five, that's a very good start."

"I agree, but there's one little problem."

"What?"

"How do you intend to get a handwriting sample from each of them? I mean it's not like you can just walk up to them and ask them for one. Actually, maybe it is a good idea. Jim Warren said Judge Lane had to sign off on the emergency papers to have me authorized to use my aunt's bank account for paying the expenses of running the ranch. We could get a sample of her handwriting from that."

"I haven't had time to tell you that I met her today."

He raised an eyebrow and quietly said, "Kelly, how in the devil did you just happen to meet one of the suspects in this case, and you've only been in town for twenty-four hours. You never fail to amaze me."

She told him about her encounter with Judge Susan Lane at Betty's Salon a few hours earlier and how interested the judge had been in wanting to know what Mike planned on doing with the ranch. She also told him about Betty, and how everyone thought

Aunt Agnes was a multimillionaire and now Mike was too.

"You've got to be kidding about this multimillionaire stuff! Jim never specifically mentioned an amount. He told me he would get back to me as to what her investments were worth on the date of her death."

"Did you ask?"

"No. It never occurred to me. Believe me, I'm trying to deal with my aunt being murdered. The size of her financial holdings has not been in the forefront of my mind, and you know money has never been a motivating factor in my life. If it had been, I wouldn't be the sheriff of a small rural county in Oregon. It isn't the best paid profession around."

"You might want to ask the attorney for some specific figures. If it's true that she really was quite wealthy, you're going to have to make even more decisions regarding what you're going to do with everything."

"I'll call him in the morning, but I'm not sure how that would affect anything I'm doing. And if I'm considered a suspect, that would only be more of a reason for me to murder her. I can't believe I even said 'a reason for me to murder her.' I've got to find the murderer and fast, before this gets out of hand."

"Probably already is, Mike. Remember, this is a small town, and small towns love a scandal. You may have unwittingly provided one. Let's have dinner, and we can continue this conversation while we eat."

A half hour later Mike said, "Kelly, these stuffed pasta shells are delicious. You're a miracle worker. I mean who else could go into a strange kitchen and create a gourmet meal without a recipe or buying anything, just using what's on hand? Kudos, lady!"

"Thanks, now let's get back to what's important and that's getting your name cleared as a suspect. We can get the judge's handwriting from the legal papers. I was thinking maybe after the funeral I'd go to the art gallery that has your cousin's art on display and ask if I could take some pictures of one of his pieces. I could always say I wanted to show it to someone before I bought it. His signature's probably on it. That would take care of two of the five."

"You may be on to something. I could go down to the old shack and see if Gary's there. If he is I'll tell him I want him off the property and ask him to sign something. I haven't really thought it through, but if he's not home, I could probably go in and see if I could find something that has his signature on it."

"Do you think your aunt has a key to the shack?"

"If there's a lock on the door, I think she would, but it was never locked when I used to come here."

"That leaves the elusive developer and the rancher neighbor. Any thoughts on those two?"

"At the moment, no. We'll just take care of one thing at a time. At some point that developer is going to have to get in touch with me if he still wants the property. Maybe I can do something then."

He was interrupted by the doorbell ringing. He looked at his watch. "Little early for Julia and Brad, isn't it?"

"Yes. She said they'd be really late and asked me what bedroom I wanted them in. She also asked if I would leave a key under the door mat and a couple of lights on."

"I hope whoever it is doesn't plan on staying very long. I'm exhausted," he said walking over to the front door.

CHAPTER EIGHTEEN

"Who is it?" Mike asked, as the doorbell rang a second time.

"It's John Wilson, your neighbor to the south." Kelly looked at Mike and raised an eyebrow. She motioned to him that she was going in the kitchen. As she retreated into it, Mike opened the door.

"Please, come in, John. I haven't seen you in ages. How are you?"

"I'm fine, but I wanted to personally stop by and offer my condolences. Your aunt and I may have had our differences, but no one would deny that she was a great lady, truly a formidable opponent." He walked over to a chair in the living room and sat down.

"Mike, I won't mince words. Your aunt may have told you I've been offering to buy her property for years. The drought has gotten so severe I'm having trouble getting enough water for my cattle. I'm sure you remember that your aunt and uncle dammed up the stream years ago, so they wouldn't have to be reliant on the city for their water. At the time I had enough underground water on my property, and while I wasn't very happy about it, it wasn't a big deal. Now it's become a big deal. I don't know how much longer I can continue to run cattle on my ranch if I don't get some water."

"I'm sorry to hear that, John. I know the drought has affected a lot of farmers and ranchers in California. It's even beginning to have an adverse effect on the economy."

"You got that right. Like I said, I'm here to express my condolences, but I'm also here to ask you, no, to plead with you to sell the Robertson Ranch to me, or open the dam so my property can get some water. I can only hang on a few more months, but if I don't find a new source of water, I'm going to have to sell my land to a developer who wants to buy it."

"That's interesting. My aunt mentioned that a developer had been trying to buy her property and put a golf course on it. She said he was even talking about making this house into a boutique hotel. I wonder if it's the same developer."

"Probably is. It's some corporation based in San Francisco. I've met with the developer, and he told me his company wanted to put a large spa and hotel on my ranch. It might fit in with the golf course theme they want to build on your aunt's property."

"John, I'm sorry about your cattle, but I'm in no position to make any decisions for a few days. Right now I'm dealing with my aunt's death, and that's my priority. If you're interested in making an offer on this property, I'd be happy to look at it, but again, I can't make any promises. Tell you what. Our families go back a long way. Why don't you hand write an offer and give it to me. I'll sit on it for a few days and make a decision then. Would that work for you?"

"Yes, that's very fair. I'll bring it to you first thing in the morning. Thanks for listening to me, and I hope we can do business one way or another." The big suntanned rancher in the red checked shirt stood up and held out his hand. "Our great-grandparents worked together. I'd like to think we could do the same."

Mike shook his hand and said, "At this point, I don't know what I'm going to do. I've been hit with a lot in the last twenty-four hours, and I need to take some time and think about all of this. I hope you understand."

"I do, and I hope you understand how serious the water issue is to me and my cattle, not to mention my family. I don't want to be the one whose legacy it was to have to sell the family ranch that had been in the family for over a century, because I couldn't find a way to get water for the cattle."

"I understand, and I'll look forward to receiving your offer in the morning. Thank you for coming by." Mike closed the door behind John and walked into the kitchen where Kelly had been listening to the conversation.

"Well, what do you think?" he asked.

"I think it was positively brilliant of you to get him to write out the offer. One by one, we're getting the handwriting samples we need."

"I have a hard time thinking of John as a suspect, and yet he certainly has a motive, actually a very powerful one. The family ranch will have to be sold if he doesn't get water for his cattle, and he knew my aunt was never going to sell it nor was she going to release the water from the dam. Now that I'm the owner of the property, maybe he thinks he stands a better chance of convincing me. I'll be curious to see what he offers me, because I have no idea what ranch property like this is worth."

"Mike, enough thinking for tonight. You need to get some sleep. Julia, Brad, and your two step granddaughters will be here when you wake up. That means there will be a lot of energy and activity in the house tomorrow, plus we have the funeral and probably half the town coming here afterwards. Time for bed. I know your mind is spinning, but as tired as you are, I'm sure you'll fall asleep the moment your head hits the pillow. Go on up. I'm going to write a note to Julia and I'll join you in a few minutes."

She watched him as he trudged up the stairs – the weight of the world on his shoulders. A tear slid down her cheek. She let the dogs out for a few minutes and then the four of them went up the stairs to the bedroom. Just as she had predicted, Mike was in bed and already sound asleep.

I wish there was something I could do for him. He's such a good man. He doesn't deserve this. I've got to find the murderer. That will be one less thing he'll have to worry about. Sleep well, Sheriff Mike. I love you.

CHAPTER NINETEEN

The next morning as the sun began to peek through their bedroom window, Kelly rolled over and looked at Mike. His eyes were wide open. "Honey, did you get any sleep last night?"

"Yeah, but I woke up about 3:00 a.m., and I couldn't get back to sleep. I kept thinking about what I could do to clear my name and find out who killed Aunt Agnes. I remembered that Gary, the guy who lives in the shack, drives a motorcycle. I actually saw him riding it when I was at Ralph's gas station the other day. I haven't heard his motorcycle since we arrived here at the ranch. I wonder if he's moved out. I'm going down to the shack this morning after I have some coffee and see what I can find out."

"You're right. It has been very quiet the last two nights, and your aunt said she often heard screaming and people's voices late at night. She was sure the sounds were coming from his shack. Maybe he has moved out. Why don't you take Brad with you? Wouldn't hurt to have someone with you in case he's there and resistant to your request that he move out of the shack."

"You're probably right. Let's get dressed and go downstairs. I can't wait to see my new family."

When Mike married Kelly he'd been warmly embraced by her two adult children, Cash and Julia. When Julia married Brad, Mike's new family increased to include a step son-in-law and two step granddaughters. He had never had children of his own and thoroughly enjoyed his new role.

As soon as they got to the bottom of the stairs they were immediately surrounded by Julia, Brad, Ella, and Olivia, the latter two being Brad's daughters from his marriage to his first wife who had died from a cocaine overdose. Everyone was talking at once. The dogs were right in the middle, wanting to be acknowledged and petted.

"Wait a minute," Mike said, trying to bring some type of order to the chaos. "First of all, what time did you get in last night? I never even heard you."

"We got to the house about midnight," Julia said. "We were pretty tired, so we went to bed immediately, but the girls were so excited they woke us up early. They want to know when they can go to the barn and if there are any horses in the barn."

"Ella, Olivia, let me pour myself a cup of coffee, and then I'll take you out to the barn. You've met Rebel and Lady before, but this is Sam. He was my aunt's dog. And yes, there is one horse, but she's pretty old. When I used to come here, my aunt had lots of horses, but now there's just one whose name is Missy. She also used to have goats and chickens and pigs and about any other animal you can name."

"Mike," Julia said, "we all want you to know how sorry we are about your aunt. It really is a tragedy, and we're here to help however we can. She must have been quite a lady if this property is any indication. I could only see a little of it last night, but I've been looking out the windows this morning, and it looks like there's an orchard a little ways from the house. And this house! I don't think I've ever seen one that can begin to compare to it. It's much more beautiful than homes in this architectural style that I've seen in San Francisco."

"Thanks. Kelly and I are really glad you were able to come. It's comforting to have family around at a time like this." He turned to Ella and Olivia. "Ready to go to the barn?"

"Yes!" Olivia shouted excitedly. "Can the dogs come with us?"

"Of course. Let's go." The six of them walked out the back door and headed for the barn.

"Mom, how's Mike doing? I hate it when I see circles that dark around someone's eyes. He looks like he's in pain."

"He is." She told Brad and Julia about the suspects, and that there was a good chance Mike might also be considered a suspect.

"Mom, you told me on the phone that Mike was his aunt's sole beneficiary. Have you and Mike decided what you're going to do with this ranch and everything else she owned?"

"No. We're trying to deal with one thing at a time, and right now the priority is the funeral this afternoon. It's at two o'clock. Some women from the church are coming to help here at the house and set up for the reception while we're at the funeral. I guess it's a custom for everyone who attends the funeral to come to the deceased person's home afterwards. You won't believe the food that's already been brought to the house. I've completely filled the refrigerator in the kitchen as well as the one in the garage."

"When I was getting breakfast for the girls I noticed that the refrigerator seemed really full. Why don't we set up the dining room table this morning? The church women can deal with the food. They've probably had a lot more experience setting it up for a funeral reception than we have."

"Good idea. Brad, would you mind going to the shack with Mike? We don't think Gary's there, but if he is, Mike might be able to use a little help."

"Happy to do it, Kelly," the tall muscular young man said. "It will give me a chance to see more of the ranch. You know when I was growing up I used to dream of being a rancher and having a place where I could ride horses and run cattle. This place is a little beyond my dreams, but I'd love to have a chance to look at the property."

"Brad, you've never mentioned this to me. Why did you become a psychologist if you wanted to be a cowboy and have your own ranch?" Julia asked. She was a younger version of her mother with her porcelain white skin, deep green eyes, and jet black hair.

"My parents were city people and anything to do with the outdoors was beyond their comprehension. I was told I would be a psychologist from the time I was a little kid. Eventually I just gave up on the idea of becoming a cowboy."

"Well, Brad, for the next few days you can play cowboy all you want, although I don't know if Missy has been ridden in a while. We might even have to rent a horse from a neighbor so you can fulfill your boyhood dream," Kelly said laughing.

"Won't be necessary. I'll be fine just walking the land and looking at the magnificent oak trees that are on the property."

"I haven't seen it yet, but evidently Gary is living in a shack on a stream that Aunt Agnes and her husband dammed up and made into a lake so they could have their own source of water. That should be pretty."

"Looking forward to it. Kelly, I brought a dark business suit to wear to the funeral, but it occurred to me that Mike probably didn't bring one if he was just coming here to visit his aunt. Do you want me to go into town and see if I can find something for him?"

"Thanks for the offer, but this is a pretty casual little town. Actually, you could probably wear jeans and a shirt and fit right in. Mike and I discussed it last night, and he's going to wear some slacks he brought, a sport coat, and an open collar shirt. He didn't bring a tie, but I don't think one's expected here. I'm wearing a pantsuit I brought. I wasn't exactly sure what the dress code would be here in Calico Gold, but I'm finding it's very casual."

Just then the back door opened with a bang. "Dad, you won't believe it. It's a for real barn with hay and everything. Grandpa Mike let us help him feed Missy, and I even gave her a carrot," Olivia shouted in excitement.

"I petted her nose," Ella said, not to be outdone.

"Dad, can we take Sam home with us?" Olivia asked. "He's going to need a new home, and you promised that someday we could have a dog."

"Sweetheart, I was talking about a little dog. Don't forget we live in a condominium and don't even have a yard. Where would you keep him? Plus, he's a pretty big dog and being kept indoors all the time wouldn't be fair to him."

Tears welled up in Olivia's eyes. Julia walked over and hugged her. "Sweetheart, let's enjoy Sam while we're here. If I know my mom and Mike, I'm sure Sam will be well taken care of. Why don't you come with me, and we'll go look at the orchard and see what kind of fruit trees are growing there."

Placated, Olivia put her hand in Julia's. "Come on, Ella, let's go." The three of them headed out the door on their way to the orchard.

Kelly watched them go and turned to Brad. "Looks like Julia's adapting well to being a stepmother."

"Beyond well. As a matter of fact, we were going to call you and tell you that Julia's going to adopt the girls. I didn't have anything to do with it. The girls came to me one night and asked if Julia could become their real mother. I can't believe at their ages, four and six, they'd even think of something like that. I told them it was Julia's decision. They asked Julia and between her tears, she agreed. We've already started the paperwork."

Kelly walked over to Brad and hugged him. "Oh, Brad, that's wonderful news. You've done a beautiful job raising them, and I'm so glad it's worked out so well."

"I'll be back in a minute, and then I'd like to go to the shack, Brad," Mike said.

When he returned Kelly said, "Mike, I hope you have your gun.

I'd like you to take it with you."

"Great minds think alike."

"Mike," Brad said, "I have a permit to carry a gun, and I usually have one with me because in my profession you never know what's going to happen. I didn't want to go through the hassle of trying to bring it when we left home, but if you have another one, I wouldn't mind carrying it."

"You can take mine, Brad," Kelly said. "Aunt Agnes had one that I can keep with me." She opened her purse and handed it to him. He raised an eyebrow inquiringly. "Mike makes me carry one," Kelly said. "There have been a few times when I've been glad I had it."

"I think it might be better for Julia if we never had this conversation. The less I know, the less I can tell her. Okay, Mike, let's go."

CHAPTER TWENTY

"Mike, how many acres is this property? It seems like it goes for quite a ways," Brad asked as he and Mike started walking toward the shack.

"I think it's about one hundred and fifty acres. My great-grandparents bought it around the turn of the century. They owned a couple of gold mines in the area, but when those dried up, they bought this property and began to raise cattle on it. When Aunt Agnes and Uncle Max took it over, they not only had cattle, they had quite a few horses and about every other animal that you'd find on a farm. I remember having fresh eggs for breakfast that my aunt had collected from the henhouse that morning. The two of them were pretty self-sufficient. They had their own water from the dammed up stream, meat from the animals, fruit from the orchards, and fresh produce from those two greenhouses you can see over there. Aunt Agnes had a real green thumb. They always had fresh vegetables and fruit. I suppose it many ways it was an idyllic life."

"Well, it's always been my dream to grow my own fruits and vegetables and have a lot of animals," Brad said. "I feel so much more alive when I'm outside and communing with nature than I do when I'm locked in my cubicle of an office listening to people tell me their problems. Don't get me wrong, I really care about my patients, but if I had a choice, believe me, my choice would be to spend my life outdoors."

"I suppose you can take comfort in the fact that you have a successful practice, and you're good at what you do. Look over there. You can see the stream and the little shack right beside it. That's where Gary lives." He told Brad about playing cowboy there when he was a young boy and visiting his aunt and uncle.

"Let's stop here for a minute. I want to see if we can hear any sounds coming from the shack. I can see Gary's motorcycle, and I find that a little strange."

Brad turned towards him. "Why is that strange?"

"Well, my aunt talked about how he rode it in the middle of the night, and it woke her up. I also heard it when I first drove into town night before last. Why it's strange is that I haven't heard it once since then. He must not have left the shack since Kelly and I got here. Okay, let's walk on over to the front of the shack, and I'm going to knock on the door. I don't see a lock, and I couldn't find a key. Why don't you stand behind me? I'd like you to keep your gun drawn, because I really don't know what to expect."

They walked through the undergrowth to the cabin, and Mike knocked on the door. There was no sound from within, and no one came to the door. He knocked again, loudly, and said in a loud voice, "Gary, it's Agnes' nephew, Mike Reynolds. Please open up."

Again, there was nothing. He quietly said to Brad, "I'm going in. Keep me covered. Something doesn't seem right."

He opened the door and yelled, "Oh no!" Brad was right behind him. They both looked in shock at the man on the floor, lying in a pool of blood, a gun in his hand. "Mike, it looks like he's committed suicide."

"Yes, it does. Don't touch anything. Did you bring a phone?"

"Here," Brad said, handing it to Mike who called 911 and explained to the dispatcher what they had found. She said the police would be there shortly.

"Brad, I've got to call Kelly and tell her what's happened. She's going to freak out if police cars come roaring up the lane." He called her and told her about Gary and asked her to point the police in the direction of the shack.

"Mike, I think you might want to look at this." Brad said, handing him a piece of paper which Mike quickly scanned.

"It's a suicide note," Mike said. "He says he couldn't take it anymore, and that he was afraid he'd hurt somebody. It says to look at the newspaper article next to the note. It will explain what he's been going through." Mike walked over to the table where Brad had found the note and saw the newspaper article. He quickly scanned it and said, "It's about a man who was diagnosed with paranoid schizophrenia. Gary must have thought he had the same thing. That would explain the screaming that Aunt Agnes heard coming from here. Poor guy. I feel sorry for him."

Mike heard voices and recognized one of them as being Chief Robbins' voice. He walked out of the shack. "Well, Chief, two deaths in the two days since I've been here. Not a very good track record, I admit, and we're still no closer to discovering who killed Aunt Agnes. If it was Gary, we'll never know."

"Mike, you know the drill. Tell me everything you can."

An hour later, the chief said, "Go on back to the house. I imagine you have a few things to do before the service this afternoon. I'm going to copy this note and send it, along with the Judge's signature, to my friend in Sacramento who's the handwriting expert."

"Chief, would you hold off? I think I'll have another one for you a little later. Might as well send them all in at once."

"Want to tell me about it?"

"I will later. If you would hold those two for now, I'd appreciate it."

"No problem. I'll be at the house after the service. If you have it, I can pick it up then."

"Thanks," Mike said, looking at Gary's body as it was being loaded into the rear of the coroner's van. "Poor guy. Served his country and then his life ends in this little run-down shack. I can't help but think he wound up ending his life because our country never adequately took care of the men we sent to Vietnam. Maybe if he'd gotten some proper mental health care for his condition his life would have been different." He sadly shook his head from side to side, and then he and Brad quietly walked back to the house.

CHAPTER TWENTY-ONE

"Mike, did Gary really commit suicide?" Kelly asked when he'd returned to the house and told her the details of what he and Brad had found at the shack.

"Yes. He left a note saying he couldn't take it anymore, and he was afraid he was going to hurt somebody. The note said the newspaper article that was next to it would explain what he'd been going through. Evidently he suffered from paranoid schizophrenia, or at least thought he did. The note didn't indicate whether it was a self-diagnosis or if he'd actually been diagnosed with that condition by a professional."

"Interesting that he wrote he was afraid he was going to hurt somebody. What do you make of that?"

"I don't know. I suppose it's quite possible he was the one who murdered Aunt Agnes. The note he left indicates he was afraid he was going to hurt somebody. Maybe if he did murder her he was afraid he would do it again. That could have been the motive for his decision to take his own life. We'll know more after the handwriting analyst examines his writing to see if there's a match to the letters Aunt Agnes received. If there's no match from him, but if there is a match with one of the others, that will be interesting information."

"What's this about a handwriting analyst?" Kelly asked.

"The chief is going to send a copy of the suicide note and the judge's handwriting to a friend he has in Sacramento who is with the Department of Justice to see if the handwriting on either one matches the letters that were sent to Aunt Agnes. I told him I was expecting to get one more sample of handwriting I'd like to have analyzed and asked him to hold off sending it to Sacramento until later today. Has John been here yet?"

"Yes. He was here about half an hour ago and left an envelope for you. He asked me to tell you he understands it will be a few days before you can get back to him and respond to his offer to buy the Robertson Ranch. Here it is." She handed him a large manila envelope.

Mike's eyes widened as he read the offer John had submitted to buy the ranch. "Wow. This property is worth a whole lot more than I thought. He's offering me two million for the ranch acreage, plus an additional two million for the Robertson House."

"You're kidding! If he's willing to offer you that much, I wonder what the developer will offer for it. That's a lot of money to turn down. Looks like you're going to have to make some tough decisions pretty soon."

"I didn't expect any of this. I really never thought about who might get the ranch when Aunt Agnes died or what might happen to it. I'm going to do something I learned to do long ago when I was dealing with very difficult cases. When I started out with the Sheriff's Department, the sheriff told me I should compartmentalize things in my mind. In other words I should do the most obvious thing at that moment and put the other things on hold. In my mind I've always referred to it as a 'NMOT' which stands for the next most obvious thing. It's really helped me from getting sidetracked during an investigation and spending a lot of wasted time on less important things. Guess the NMOT now is Aunt Agnes' funeral. How about making me a little lunch and then we probably better go to the church and get this thing over with?"

"Couldn't help but overhear that, Mike," Julia said. "That's something I'm capable of doing. I'll make lunch, and we can all go together when we leave for the funeral. Brad rented a van for our drive over from San Francisco, so there's plenty of room." A few minutes later she called out, "Lunch is ready, and I'm serving it on the porch. I could use a couple of hands to help me carry everything out there."

The two young girls ate quickly and asked to be excused so they could go see Missy in the barn. When they were out of earshot, Brad said, "I think we need to say something to the girls about Gary's death, but I'm just not sure what. I'm afraid they'll hear something when people come to the house after the funeral. There's bound to be a lot of talk about it, and I imagine a few people will step outside and try to take a look at the shack."

"I agree," Julia said. "I'll just tell them it was very sad that Grandpa and Dad found a man who had died when they were on their walk this morning. That should satisfy them. I think they're far more interested in Missy and Sam. When I get them dressed, I'll mention it, which it's about time to do right now."

"Julia, Brad, I'll clean up while you're getting the girls ready. Mike, why don't you take a shower, and I'll be up in a few minutes to get dressed," Kelly said.

"Thanks, there's something about death that always makes me feel unclean, but you know that," Mike said.

"Yes, exactly why I suggested it. I suppose the silver lining is that you don't have to get into some sort of confrontation trying to get Gary to leave the shack."

"No, he took care of that for me," Mike said, as he started to walk up the stairs.

This will keep the town gossips busy for a while, Kelly thought. *Another death here at the ranch, and we still don't know who killed Aunt Agnes. That's got to be the NMOT for me to do once her funeral is over. I might even have time to get to the art gallery late this afternoon and see if I can get a copy of Daniel's handwriting. If not, I definitely need to do it first thing in the morning.*

CHAPTER TWENTY-TWO

"Mike, just a few more hours, and this will all be behind you. I want you to know I'm right here for you. You're not going through this alone," Kelly said, kissing him lightly on the cheek as they got ready to go downstairs and meet the rest of the family.

"Thanks, sweetheart. It's just that I've been flooded with a lot of childhood memories from the past. I can't help but think that this is the end of line for the Reynolds branch of the family. I'm the last one, and I don't have any children. There's no one left after me. One way or another at some point in time this beautiful old ranch will fall into the hands of someone other than a family member. I've never thought about it before, but now I feel like I've let everyone down. It's so sad to think that my aunt loved this town and this ranch so much she was willing to fight to protect it and then was murdered, possibly because of her love for the town and the ranch. I really don't know what to do. I'm almost overwhelmed by the whole situation."

"Remember what you told me earlier about the NMOT. Right now the next most obvious thing is getting you through this funeral, and Mike, you're the one who's usually very pragmatic. You, more than anyone else, should know this will all be resolved in time, and I guarantee you it will be for the best. I believe that, and I hope you will too."

"Ah, Kelly, what would I do without you? I don't say it often enough, but there's no doubt in my mind that you're the best thing that ever happened to me. Thank you."

"Sheriff, the pleasure is all mine, but I'll be just as glad as you will when this is all over."

*****

The minister had told them to meet him in his office, so they could enter the front pew from the side of the church rather than having to walk down the aisle.

As Kelly walked beside Mike to take her seat, she quickly glanced towards the rear of the church. It was completely filled, and people were standing along the sides and at the rear.

I don't know if this is because Aunt Agnes was so highly regarded or because two deaths took place in two days on her property. I'm going for the high road here and hope it's the former.

Kelly thought the service was lovely, from the warm off-the-cuff talk the minister gave about the life of Agnes Johnson to the ending hymn, Amazing Grace, which was sung beautifully by a member of the church choir. The family left the church by the back entrance and quietly got into Brad's van. Kelly put her hand on Mike's as he looked out the window on the drive back to the ranch, doing his best to fight back tears for the loss of his beloved Aunt Agnes. No one spoke during the short drive. Ella and Olivia were uncommonly quiet, sensing the solemnness of what had occurred at the church.

Several of the ladies from the church had come to the house just as the family was leaving for the funeral. They told Mike they were sure his aunt would understand why they weren't at the funeral, and that they needed to get ready for the people who would be coming to the ranch after the funeral. When they drove down the lane on their return to the Robertson House, Kelly and Mike noticed that several more cars were there. Fortunately with a ranch as large as the Robertson Ranch, parking wasn't a problem.

Kelly walked into the kitchen and introduced herself to the

women she hadn't met. "Thank you all so much for doing this. You've done a beautiful job, and the lemonade is a perfect choice for a warm day like today. I have no idea how many people will show up, but be forewarned, the church was standing room only."

"Honey," the large woman with the apron tied around her generous midsection said, "you can plan on just about everybody in town coming. News of the second death makes this the place to be today. This town has never had a murder before, and I don't remember ever hearing about a suicide. Yes, this is where it's at today.

"We've got a load of food here, but I just hope it's enough. When this is over, your face is going to hurt from smiling, and your hand is going to hurt from shaking everybody else's hand. Better get ready. Looks like the first ones are coming up the lane as I speak. By the way, I make a cake for occasions like this that I call 'The Big Smile Cake.' I named it that because if nothing else, it brings a smile to people's faces during tragic times, and we can all use a few happy faces on a sad day like today. I'm going to save a piece and put it in the refrigerator for you."

"I could use something to smile about. Knowing it's in the refrigerator will help me make it through the next few hours. Thank you so much."

CHAPTER TWENTY-THREE

The first person Mike saw when he got back to the house after the funeral service was Ralph, the gas station owner he talked to when he'd first come to town. As soon as he stepped out of the van, Ralph quickly walked over to him.

"Mike, sorry to intrude on yer' privacy before everyone comes here from the funeral, but I really need to talk to ya'. I think it's important."

Mike turned to Kelly and said, "Would you mind greeting the first people who get here? Ralph wants to talk to me. He says it's important."

"Of course not." She walked over to Ralph and extended her hand. "Hi, I'm Kelly, Mike's wife. Thanks for coming. By the way, I love your gas station." She turned away and introduced herself to the mourners who were beginning to arrive at the ranch.

"Could we go out back and sit on the patio?" Ralph asked. "Agnes and I used to sit there when we were plannin' what we were gonna talk 'bout before each of our weekly meetins'. What I want to tell you's private, so I'd jes' as soon not have a lot of people breathin' down my neck, and from the looks of the traffic coming up the lane, it's going to get real crowded real soon."

"Of course. Follow me," Mike said, as he walked through the house and out the sliding glass doors that led to the patio. He walked over to a small table that was hidden from the house by a large oak tree that the patio had been built around. When they were both seated, he looked at Ralph and said, "We can talk privately here."

"Mike, I knew yer' aunt all my life. I'm only a few years younger than she was, and I was a good friend of yer' uncle's. I remember when they took the Robertson Ranch over from her parents. Max was a real environmentalist before anyone knew what the word meant, and Agnes was only 'bout half a step behind him. When Max decided to do what they call nowadays, 'live off the grid,' she was all for it. They both had a real independent streak in them and wanted to be able to have everything they needed to live on available from the ranch, as best they could. Didn't want to be beholden to the city of Calico Gold if they could help it. Course they couldn't do much about electricity."

"When I used to come here as a child," Mike said, "Aunt Agnes always told me never to rely on anyone else. She told me that was the reason she and Uncle Max lived like they did with all of the plants and animals. I believe that was the reason they dammed up the stream."

"Yeah, I remember when they did it. John Wilson was madder than a hornet. His family had been gettin' water from the stream on the Robertson Ranch ever since either ranch had been there. At the time he had a lot of underground water, so it wasn't a real big deal, but he still didn't like it. Mike, mind if I have a smoke? I'm a little nervous tellin' you 'bout this, and it'd make me feel better."

"No, go ahead. We're outside, and I'm sure there will be others this afternoon who will step outside for a smoke."

Ralph lit a Camel cigarette and inhaled deeply. "Don't know what 'tis about these dang things that make me feel better, but they do. Okay, back to what I was jawin' 'bout. Max and John had an argument 'bout dammin' up the stream. Max told me 'bout it and then a few days later, John was gassin' up his pickup, and he tol' me 'bout it. I'm still the only gas station for miles around, so I hear things you wouldn't believe."

"I'm sure you do. My wife has a small coffee shop in Cedar Bay, Oregon, where we live. Everyone comes to the coffee shop to find out the latest rumors. I imagine your gas station is about the same."

"That it is. Only other place around where people like to jaw is at Betty's Salon. Between us we probably know everything that's goin' on in Calico Gold. Anyway that was a lot of years ago, but every time John comes to the station he still says somethin' about that dam. Don't think he and Max ever spoke to each other again. During the last few years with the drought and all, he's gotten even angrier. Hear he's afraid he's gonna run out of water, and them cattle he's got will all die. Agnes told me several times he'd offered her a lot of money for the ranch, but she'd promised Max she wouldn't sell it, and she was bound and determined to keep that promise. Kind of surprised me, her being such an animal lover and all. Guess she had a blind spot when it came to that dam. Anyway that's the background."

"Yes, she told me pretty much the same thing."

"Well, here's what she didn't tell ya'," he said, looking around to make sure no one was listening. He needn't have worried. No one was on the patio. "John came into the station the other day, and I was all geared up to listen to him jaw 'bout how yer' aunt wouldn't sell him the ranch, sayin' the same old things he always did. Instead, he was all smiles. Asked him what the big smile was all about, and he says to me, 'Ralph, that ranch is gonna be mine. Got it figured out how I can get it. Can't say more than that, but I'm gonna be a happy man real soon and so are my cattle.' That's what he said." Ralph sat back and looked at Mike.

"What do you think he meant?" Mike asked. "Did he say anything else?"

"Asked him that very question. Said somethin' 'bout not bein' at liberty or some such thing to say anything more, but everything was gonna be jes' fine real soon."

"Ralph, you wouldn't come out here and tell me this if you didn't have some thoughts on it. So let me ask you again, what do you think he meant?"

He was quiet for a long time, and then he said, "Don't ya' think it's kind of a coincidence, him sayin' that and yer' aunt being murdered in the barn? It was pretty common knowledge that Agnes went out to the barn early every mornin' to groom and feed Missy. Kinda convenient, his ranch bein' so close, like right next to the Robertson Ranch. Funny thing is he's got a strip of his ranch that ain't too far from the barn. Always did think it was strange to have that one strip of his property there. It's kind of like a finger that protrudes into the Robertson Ranch. Asked Max 'bout it once, and he said the families who owned both of the ranches before the Wilsons and yer' aunt's family had been related and wanted to be near each other. Guess at one time there was even a little house on that finger of land, but that's long gone."

"I've never heard anything about that. I thought all of the property surrounding the house and the barn was part of the Robertson Ranch."

"Tis ceptin' for that little strip I jes' told you 'bout. Don't look no different than yer' aunt's property, but if ya' look real close you'll see there's a tree line that Agnes planted, so she wouldn't have to look at that section of land. It's probably less than a hundred yards from that little strip of land to where the barn's located and those trees Agnes planted years ago. Well, guess what? They block out any clear vision a person might have lookin' out from the house towards John's ranch. Seems to me it would be pretty easy fer' someone to sneak undetected into the barn from John's nearby property. Anyway, thought ya' oughta know 'bout it. Ain't accusin' nobody, jes' sayin' ya' might wanna think 'bout it."

"Thanks, Ralph, I will. I really appreciate your coming out here and telling me. I don't know what to make of it. I know that John wants the ranch, in fact, he's offered to buy it from me, but a piece of his land being that close to the barn? That's complete news to me."

"Probably would be to most people. 'Member a night when I was here fer' dinner, and we had a long talk about it. Yer' aunt and Max didn't like it, but there weren't nothin' they could do 'bout it. I've been jawin' at ya' long enough. Sounds like a lot of people are here. If ya' need anything, gimme a call. Kind of feel like yer' family, being Agnes' nephew and all," he said as he stood up. "One more thing, son, be careful. From what I hear, the ranch is yours. If someone killed Agnes to get it, ya' might be next. Make sure ya' got yer' back covered."

"I will, and thanks again, Ralph."

CHAPTER TWENTY-FOUR

The next three hours passed by in a blur for Kelly and Mike. She was glad Julia and Brad had come to help out. Kelly felt like she was on display in the window of a department store, an object everyone wanted to look at and inspect. She could tell by the way people were looking at Mike that some of them considered him a suspect in the death of Aunt Agnes. It was not a good feeling.

She felt a tap on her shoulder and turned around. "Mrs. Reynolds," Judge Lane said, "I want to introduce you to Richard Martin. He came from San Francisco to attend the service. He's a developer there and someone who's very interested in acquiring the Robertson Ranch."

Kelly shook his hand and said, "It's nice to meet you. Thank you for coming."

"It was a beautiful service. I never had the pleasure of meeting Agnes, but one of my associates did on several occasions. I wanted to buy this property, but Agnes couldn't bring herself to sell it. Now that she's deceased, I understand from Judge Lane that your husband has inherited it. I'd like to talk to him, but I realize this isn't the proper time or place. I'm spending the night at the Gold Dust Bed and Breakfast Inn. Is there any chance I could meet with him in the morning?"

"I can't speak for him, and I don't know what his plans are for the ranch. Why don't you give me your cell phone number, and if he isn't able to meet with you, I'll have him call you. If you don't hear from him, plan on coming out here to the ranch around ten tomorrow morning."

"That would work fine for me. I'm looking forward to meeting your husband and talking to him." The two of them turned away from Kelly and walked down the steps to his car, a silver Lexus.

People were gradually beginning to leave, and Kelly and Mike were standing on the porch thanking them for coming when suddenly a pick-up truck raced up the lane and screeched to a stop in front of the Robertson House. A man staggered out of the truck with a gun in his hand and said in a loud slurring voice, "Where's Mike Reynolds? I wanna personally thank him for stealing from me what I shouldda' rightfully had."

Mike stepped away from Kelly and said, "I'm Mike Reynolds. Who are you, and what in the devil do you think you're doing with that gun in your hand?"

Kelly noticed that the police chief and two of his men were quickly making their way towards the intruder.

"I'm the one that shouldda' gotten this house and the ranch property," the man yelled. "Name's Daniel Noonan. I'm Agnes Johnson's nephew. My mother was her sister. Probably don't mean much to you, cuz it sure didn't mean nothing to your mother and your grandparents. Kicked my mother out of the house like she was a piece of trash and never had nothin' to do with either one of us. Yep, this property should be mine, not yours."

He turned and looked at the people who were standing on the porch and the lawn staring at him in open-mouthed disbelief. "See this man, the one who's name is Mike Reynolds? Well, you're lookin' at my aunt's murderer. He's the one who killed her, so he could get his hands on the Robertson Ranch. You wanna solve this case Chief Robbins? Don't need to look no farther. Jes' arrest him right here and now and cart him off to jail where he belongs."

Daniel tried to whirl around to face the police chief who was rapidly approaching, but because of his obvious drunken condition, he lost his balance and fell to the ground. He dropped the gun in his hand when he hit the ground. Chief Robbins scooped up the gun and one of his deputies subdued Daniel and handcuffed him.

The chief looked at the people who were staring at what was taking place and said, "Show's over, folks. Go on back in the house or home. We're going to take Daniel for a little ride, and he'll be cooling his heels in jail until the alcohol wears off. Nothing more to see here." He walked over to Mike and said, "I'll be back a little later. I'm going to book him for disturbing the peace. When he sobers up, I'll probably let him go, but not until I impound that pistol he was waving around. I'll find some way to get some handwriting from him. You mentioned you might have one more for me. Do you?"

"Yes."

"Good, I'll get it when I come back. Try to forget what he said. I'm sure it was the alcohol talking, not him. By the way, haven't had a chance to tell you, but I ran a fingerprint test on those letters that were sent to your aunt and there weren't any prints on them other than hers."

"Thanks, and I'm not so sure it was just the alcohol talking. From the looks I've been getting from some of the folks who are here today, he's not the only one in town who thinks I may be the one who killed Aunt Agnes."

"All the more reason to find the killer. We need to clear your name. Just for the record, Mike, I believe you."

"I appreciate that. See you later."

Kelly walked over to Mike and put her hand on his arm. "You okay, honey?"

"Yeah. Just didn't need that right now. Our trip to see Aunt Agnes is becoming one big nightmare. It seems like it's just one ugly thing after another."

"We'll get through it. I'm right here for you and so are Brad and Julia. You're not going through this by yourself."

"Thanks. Don't worry about me. I'll be fine."

"I know you'll be fine, but I do worry about you, and from the way Rebel's looking at you, he's worried too." They both turned to look down at the big boxer who was standing as close to Mike as he could get. It was as if he was trying to protect him from everything that was happening.

"Kelly, did you notice if Rebel was standing next to me when Daniel started yelling at me?"

"I was watching Daniel. People with guns scare me, particularly drunk people with guns. Knowing Rebel, I imagine he sensed danger and probably came up to you about that time. The last time I remember seeing him, he was in the yard with Sam and Lady and now here he is right next to you. I think he constantly watches out for you."

Mike reached down and scratched Rebel's ears. "Thanks, big guy. I'm fine, but it sure makes me feel good to know you're here for me."

Kelly walked into the kitchen to thank the ladies from the church. "I really appreciate everything you've done today. I don't know what I would have done without you. People are leaving, and it looks like the fireworks are over, so why don't you go ahead and take off. My daughter and I can clean up everything that's left."

"Kelly," the large woman who had spoken to Kelly earlier said, "there's not much to clean up other than a few pots and pans. It's a good thing so many people brought food, because we've put out the last of it."

"That's amazing! I thought we'd be eating that food for days."

"Nope. Since we used paper plates and cups, shouldn't be too bad of a clean-up job. How's your husband doing? Shame that cousin of his had to barge in here and say those awful things about him. Don't think people will pay him much mind. He's not too well-liked around these parts."

"Thanks. My husband is fine. It's just that a day like today is stressful enough without adding something to it like what just happened. I know Mike will be very glad when the killer is finally found."

"He's not the only one. A lot of us are locking our doors and looking over our shoulders when we walk down the street. We're not used to a murderer being on the loose in Calico Gold. All of us hope he or she is found real soon. And Kelly, remember that I saved you a piece of my Big Smile cake. It's in the refrigerator."

"Thanks. Again, I really appreciate everything you've done."

The ladies from the church were soon gone. There had been enough going on at Aunt Agnes' funeral and reception to keep every gossip in town busy for a long time.

CHAPTER TWENTY-FIVE

The funeral service and reception that followed had made it an exhausting day, and everyone in the family was tired. After finishing dinner they sat on the porch, quietly letting the events of the day drift away. Mike was sitting on the porch swing with Ella and Olivia next to him, while he pointed to different stars in the sky and called out their names. If one could ignore the fact that there had been two recent deaths on the ranch, it easily could have been a scene taken from an old Norman Rockwell painting. Unfortunately the two deaths took away the serenity of the moment.

"Mike, someone's coming up the lane. I can see the headlights," Brad said.

"Swell, that's just what I need. You'd think whoever it is would realize we've had a rough day and give us a little privacy. I'm not up to making nice one more time." He stood and walked to the edge of the porch.

A dark blue pickup truck pulled up in front of the porch, and a man about forty years old got out. His black hair was beginning to grey at the temples, and he was dressed in blue jeans, a light blue chambray shirt, and wore cowboy boots. "You must be Mike Reynolds," he said, holding out his hand. "I'm Huston Brooks. I want to apologize for not being able to attend your aunt's funeral today, but I was in court all day."

"My aunt talked to me about you, and how she was supporting you in your campaign to be elected judge. Let me introduce you to my family."

Huston walked up the steps and shook hands with everyone as Mike made the introductions.

"Mike, I feel like I know you because your aunt spoke so highly of you. She told me she'd called and asked you to come to the ranch. Agnes told me about some letters she'd recently received, and I became concerned for her safety. I urged her to tell the police chief about them, but your aunt was not the easiest person to persuade if her mind was set against something. She was certain you could help, and she told me she'd wait until you got here before deciding what to do about the letters."

"I wish she'd listened to you, Huston. If she had, maybe she wouldn't have been murdered. I feel certain there must be a connection between the letters she received and her murder. The night before she was murdered she told me about several people she thought might have sent them."

"I have some ideas on that subject. Let's compare notes."

"Please tell me. I want to get this behind me, plus there's one other problem. I'm considered by some to be a suspect, because my aunt made me the sole beneficiary of her Will. I had no idea she was even thinking of something like that. I not only want to catch the killer, I want to clear my name."

"For one," Huston said, "I never trusted the guy, Gary Sanders, who was living in the shack next to the stream on the ranch. I understand he committed suicide this morning, and I told your aunt repeatedly that something was really wrong with him. He certainly would be a suspect in my eyes."

"Yes, he was in my mind too. I realize he could have done it, but in a suicide note he left he said that's why he was committing suicide, so he wouldn't hurt anyone. It's a bit of a paradox, and if he was the killer, I don't know how we could prove it now that he's dead."

"I know you'll think what I'm about to say is self-serving, but I have strong doubts about Judge Lane and a developer by the name of Richard Martin. I know she's gotten over $60,000 in campaign contributions from him, and they both wanted to see this property developed. What stood in the way was your aunt."

"Yes, I'm very aware of their relationship. They were at the funeral, and as a matter of fact, I have a meeting with Richard Martin tomorrow morning here at the ranch."

"I got a call from my campaign consultant on the way over here. He's been investigating Martin, and evidently his company has been involved in several things which were illegal, but the company has always managed to skate. According to him, the judge and Martin are involved in more than a platonic relationship. She's been able to help him gain approval for a number of his projects, some of which probably never should have been approved. In her capacity as judge, she's overridden certain county requirements such as building setbacks, water rights, parking requirements, and evidently quite a few others. Whether the two of them would go as far as murder? Who knows? But what is known is that they have a history of turning their backs on the law in order to get what they want. In my opinion both of them are arrogant and ambitious."

"Thanks for sharing your thoughts with me. On a similar subject, do you know if John Wilson, the rancher who owns the ranch adjacent to the Robertson Ranch, and Richard Martin have any type of a relationship?"

"I asked my consultant to look into that as well, because I know your aunt always wondered if that was one of the reasons John wanted to buy her ranch. He couldn't find anything that linked the two of them together other than Martin, the developer, had offered to buy Wilson's land. It looks like Martin wants the Robertson Ranch for the golf course and John's property for the resort. Since they're adjoining properties, it would make sense. John's always been a straight shooter in my book. I've never known him to do anything illegal. I truly think he wants the Robertson Ranch for the water, and nothing else."

"That was my impression. He told me he didn't want it to be his legacy that he had to sell his ranch, which had been in his family for over a hundred years, because he couldn't find a way to get water onto the property. I would do the same if I was him, but then again, he's desperate, and desperate men are often pushed to do things they would never normally do."

"Sounds like you've been able to come up with several suspects. Any more?"

"Yes. My aunt told me the night I arrived about a cousin I have by the name of Daniel Noonan. I previously knew nothing about him, but apparently she told him recently he would not be inheriting the property, and that I was the sole beneficiary of her Will. She told me he was very angry, and he made a scene here today during the reception which followed the funeral. He didn't actually threaten me, but he was drunk and waving a gun around. The chief arrested him. He's in jail at the moment."

"Your aunt told me about him, and how she'd been supporting him for years. She said she knew she should stop, but she still felt guilty about what her parents had done to your aunt's sister. I've met him a couple of times, and I didn't like him. As a matter of fact, I told your aunt I thought she should cut him off. She listened to me, but I don't think she heard me."

"The police chief believes in my innocence. He and I have managed to get handwriting samples from all of the people I've mentioned with the exception of Richard Martin, the developer. I'll try to think of something I can have him sign when he's here tomorrow. The chief has a friend in Sacramento who's with the Department of Justice, and his specialty is handwriting analysis. According to the chief, he's been used as an expert witness in a lot in court cases. We're hoping there's a match between one of the suspect's handwriting and the letters. That's a place to start. It won't prove who murdered Aunt Agnes, but it would show who sent her the letters. At least we'd be one step closer to finding out who did it."

"I think that's an excellent plan. What can I do to help?"

"Nothing that I can think of. By the way, I'd like to make a contribution to your campaign, and I believe Kelly, Brad, and Julia would like to as well." He turned to them. "Is that all right with all of you?"

There was a unanimous response of yes. "Why don't you give me a few campaign contribution envelopes? I think we can all write a maximum amount check to you."

"Thank you, all of you. That's an extremely generous thing for you to do. I certainly didn't come here tonight to solicit campaign funds. I came here because your aunt was my role model, and I want to do anything I can to help you find the person who killed her. If you need anything, please call me. Here's my business card, and my cell phone number is on the reverse side."

"My aunt believed in you, and as we all know, she didn't suffer fools lightly. I wish you the best of luck in your campaign. Thanks for coming out here. I know you must be tired. Spending a day in court, driving home, and then taking the time to come out here tells me a lot about you. Thanks again," Mike said.

"Nice meeting all of you. I'll be seeing you," Huston said as he walked down the steps and got in his truck. He waved one final time and then drove down the lane.

"Nice man," Kelly said. "That was a class act to come out here after his long day. No wonder your aunt was helping him. I hope he wins the election. Certainly seems like his character is a lot better than the judge's."

"Couldn't agree more, sweetheart. I've got to get some sleep. A major case of fatigue is visiting me, and it looks like it's settled in for the night."

Julia stood up. "I think we're all ready for a good night of sleep. Come on girls. Mom, see you in the morning," she said as she kissed Kelly on the cheek and took the girls' hands.

"You all go on up. I'll let the dogs out and lock up. Sleep well," Brad said as the rest of them walked up the stairs, hoping for a better night's sleep than the one they'd had the night before.

CHAPTER TWENTY-SIX

Kelly woke up with a start in the middle of the night, trying to capture what she'd been dreaming about. She remembered she and Mike were talking about how the police chief had four samples of handwriting and was going to send them to his friend in Sacramento. She'd reminded Mike that the developer, Richard Martin, was coming to the Robertson House at ten the next morning. Mike had said something about trying to get a sample of his handwriting, but he couldn't think of any reason the developer would give it to him.

Like a spark plug firing off in her brain, Kelly thought if the judge and the developer had gone to Aunt Agnes' funeral, which they surely must have given the fact they showed up at the reception, maybe they signed the guest book that was usually kept in the area outside the church sanctuary. Kelly hadn't been in the front entrance area of the church during the funeral service, so she wasn't sure if there had even been a guest book, but it was the traditional thing to do. She decided to go to the church first thing in the morning to see if Richard Martin had signed the guest book.

If he signed the guest book, and I can get a copy of it, we'll have the handwriting of all five of the suspects. It doesn't put a smoking gun in any of their hands, but if there's a match, it's a start. With that thought in mind, she drifted off to sleep.

Early the next morning Kelly said, "Mike, I'm going into town and get a couple of things. I should be back before Richard Martin gets here. I've run out of milk, and you know how much the girls drink. See you in a little while."

She drove into Calico Gold, once again charmed by the quaint beauty of the small town. She felt sorry for the townspeople knowing that the murder of Aunt Agnes had them spooked. The town they'd always looked upon as the safest place in the world didn't seem quite so safe now.

Kelly pulled into the church parking lot, surprised to see a number of cars already parked there. They'd parked behind the church yesterday, and she'd missed the big nursery school sign prominently displayed on the building next to the church.

Ah, that's why there are so many cars here this early in the morning. They have a nursery school, and that means there will probably be someone in the church business office.

She knocked on the door with the word "Office" on it and opened it. An older woman sat at a desk in front of a computer. "May I help you?" the woman asked, turning towards Kelly.

"Yes. A funeral for my husband's aunt was held here yesterday. I was wondering if a guest book had been signed by people attending the funeral."

"Of course, but first of all, let me express my condolences. I was at the funeral and also at the ranch house. I'm so sorry about Agnes. She was a wonderful woman, and I'm also sorry for what your husband must be going through. What happened with his cousin was horrible. To be grieving and then have his cousin publicly accuse him of being responsible for Agnes' murder was unforgiveable. He certainly didn't seem to be grieving. I'm just glad Agnes didn't see that. What can I help you with?"

"My husband would like to see the guest book. There were so many people at the funeral he can't even begin to remember who was there. I don't know what your church's policy is regarding releasing the guest book to the family. Would it be possible for me to take it to him? If you need it returned to the church, I'd be happy to bring it back later today."

"Oh, that's not a problem. We usually give it to the family. I don't know why it wasn't given to you yesterday. I'm not sure where it is. Let me go look for it."

A few minutes later she returned, the book in her hand. "I'm sorry, but evidently we had a woman overseeing the signing of the book who had never done it before, and she put it on the shelf under the podium that was used for signing. Here, it's yours to keep. I'm glad you thought to ask about it. I don't know how long it would have stayed there."

"Thank you so much. You've been very helpful. I really appreciate it," Kelly said as she took the offered book and smiled at the lady.

"Please tell your husband we're so sorry for his loss."

"I will, and thank you again."

Kelly walked out the door and headed towards her car. It took every bit of willpower she possessed to make it to the car without opening the book to see if Richard Martin had signed it. She left the church parking lot, drove two blocks, and pulled over to the curb. There, on the fourth page of the book written with a flourish of self-importance was the signature of Richard Martin.

Finally, we're getting a break. About time. Better head over to the police chief's office. Maybe I can get the book to him before he sends those other signatures to Sacramento.

A few minutes later she asked the person working at the front desk in the police station if Chief Robbins would have time to see Kelly Reynolds for just a moment. The young man called the chief and directed her to an office down the hall. On the door were the words "Police Chief." She walked into an office where two police officers were sitting at a desk piled high with folders. She assumed they were criminal cases, although to Kelly it seemed like a lot of cases for such a small town.

"I'm here to see Chief Robbins," she said to the young woman who looked up from the desk.

"He's in that room. Just knock and walk in. He told me he was expecting you."

"Good morning, Mrs. Reynolds. What brings you here so bright and early?"

"I had a thought in the middle of the night. I followed up on it and was able to get a sample of Richard Martin's handwriting."

"Well that's good news. How were you able to do it?"

She told him about the guest book and going to the church to get it. "I didn't tell Mike about it, because I didn't want him to be disappointed if the church hadn't used a guest book. I drove directly here in hopes you haven't sent the other handwriting samples to your friend in Sacramento."

"I'm glad you did because if you'd been a few minutes later, the signatures would have been on their way. One of my officers has to testify at a trial in Sacramento later today, and he was just getting ready to drive over there. He'll be taking the samples, and I'll add this one to it. Good thinking on your part. You thought like somebody with law enforcement experience. Do you have any training in that area?"

"Not really, however, being married to a sheriff has probably affected my way of thinking. Is this a lengthy procedure? I don't know anything about handwriting analysis."

"No. We should know something later today or tomorrow. It's really very simple. He's been trained for years in handwriting analysis. It's quite interesting. He uses the physical characteristics and patterns of the written words and letters to see if there's a match. He tells me that the handwriting often indicates the psychological state of the writer as well as some personality characteristics. He says it's very clear as to gender. In fact, a number of courts allow this type of evidence during a trial. If we get a match, we'll at least know who wrote the letters, and then we'll have to decide what our strategy will be."

"That's fascinating! I didn't know that much could be determined from a simple specimen of a person's handwriting."

"I agree. By the way, when I went back to the ranch late yesterday to get the samples that Mike had, he gave me the one from John Wilson. Sorry, but I couldn't help but notice the amount he's willing to pay for the ranch. That's a huge chunk of change. Has Mike made any decision about what he's going to do with the ranch?"

"Not that I know of. First he wanted to get through the funeral and now his focus is on clearing his name and finding out who murdered his aunt. Once those are finished, he's going to have to make some decisions regarding the ranch. We're staying here for a little while as are my daughter and son-in-law. I don't know what's going to happen after that."

"Well, you know I'm here to help in any way I can. You might tell Mike I released Daniel Noonan this morning with a strong admonition for him to keep away from Mike and the ranch. I told him if anything like that happened again, he'd be spending quite a bit of time in jail. He didn't actually threaten anyone, and he's never been in trouble with the law before, so I knew I'd have a hard time making a case against him stick. A good attorney could probably get it thrown out of court."

"I'm sorry nothing could be done about him, but I understand. I hope he stays away as well. I've got to be going, as I have to pick up some milk and get back to the ranch. Richard Martin is meeting Mike at ten this morning. I'll be curious to see what he's going to offer for the property."

"Well, whatever your husband decides to do, looks like he's a wealthy man now."

"Neither one of us ever expected this, believe me. Who would have thought the sheriff of Beaver County, Oregon, whose wife owns a small coffee shop on the pier in Cedar Bay, would suddenly be in line to receive this kind of money? Not me. Thanks for everything and we'll be waiting for your call."

CHAPTER TWENTY-SEVEN

Kelly made it back to the house a few minutes before Mike was to meet with Richard Martin. "Mike, you don't need to get a handwriting sample from Richard Martin. I was able to get one, and I've already taken it to Chief Robbins. It's on its way to Sacramento as we speak."

"You what? Kelly, you know I don't want you to get involved in this case. I can handle it."

"It was no big deal. Let me tell you what I did. I came up with the idea in the middle of the night, and it was such a simple thing." She told him about her trip to the church and her visit to the police chief.

"I don't know whether to thank you or strangle you, but given the circumstances, guess I'll just say thank you. Now all we can do is wait for the chief's phone call."

"The chief said he should find out either this afternoon or tomorrow morning, so at least we don't have to wait for days. Do you want me to be at your meeting with Richard Martin?"

"No, I think it will be a classic 'here's my offer for the property' meeting. I'll tell him the same thing I told John. I can't make any decisions until I find out who murdered my aunt. That takes precedence over everything else. Why don't you spend a little time with Julia and the girls? You don't get many chances to enjoy them. You might want to take a walk around the property. The girls have been pretty limited to the orchard and the barn. While you're at it, I'd love to know what Aunt Agnes had, if anything, growing in the greenhouses."

"From the amount of vegetables and fruits in the refrigerator, I'm pretty sure she had a bunch of things growing in them. Okay, I'll see if Julia and the girls want to do a little exploring. We'll be back in a little while. I'm pretty sure Richard Martin has only got one thing on his mind and that's getting his hands on this property. Keep in mind he could care less about Aunt Agnes."

"I'm sure you're right. I'm not deluding myself into thinking he's driving here out of fondness for Aunt Agnes. Well, speaking of the devil, he just drove up."

Mike walked over to the front door to greet Richard Martin, and Kelly went upstairs to find the rest of the family and invite them to explore the property with her.

"Richard, thank you for coming out here this morning."

"This is only my second time on the property. Yesterday at the reception following the funeral was my first. I offered to purchase it from photographs one of my staff had taken. I must say the photographs didn't do it justice. I brought some plans with me I had drawn up to show you what I have in mind. I wanted to show them to your aunt, but she refused to meet with me."

"Why don't you spread them out on the dining room table, and you can walk me through what you want to do with the property if it's developed."

Mike spent a few minutes looking at the plans and then said, "I'd like you to tell me what I'm looking at. It's kind of hard for me to understand."

"First of all, I have the plans for the golf course. I hired one of the foremost golf course designers in the United States, and these are the plans he's drawn up. I think it will become a destination golf course within a few years. I also brought the plans for the house. You can see I've added a number of rooms and expanded the dining room, so we can accommodate up to forty guests. We'll have two large dining room tables and serve the meals family style.

"Each guest room will have its own bathroom, so those need to be added as well. I'll bring in a top chef, and I'll pitch it to the 'foodie' crowd. There are currently two existing greenhouses on the property. I'll expand those so part of the draw will be that all the vegetables and herbs served with the meals are grown on the property as well as fruit from the orchards."

"What are you going to do about the lake?"

"It will be stocked with fish, and that will be another selling point. While the golfers are on the course, the rest of the family can fish in the lake or else swim in the Olympic size pool I'm going to build. There will also be excursions to nearby wineries and gold mines located in the area. I intend to purchase John Martin's property and build a large spa and resort on it. There will be plenty for people who stay at either place to do, but I've saved the best for last."

"What's that?" Mike asked.

"I'm going to make the barn into an event center. Weddings held in barns are really big right now. We can hold business meetings in there as well as other types of social events. Should be a real money maker."

"One of the things my aunt loved about this property was the number of old oak trees on it. Do you have any plans to preserve them?"

"No. They're going to have to be cut down. Might keep a couple to make the golf course interesting, but almost all of them are going to have to go. They'll just be in the way of the development."

"I don't know what this property is zoned for. Will it be a problem to get it rezoned if you have to?"

"No. I have my sources, and they're very helpful when it comes to little things like that. I don't anticipate any problems. Here's the offer I've prepared," Richard Martin said, handing an envelope to Mike. "How long do you think it will take you to accept it?"

"You're assuming that I'm going to agree to sell this property to you."

"Of course I am. You'd be a fool not to accept my offer. Now that the old lady is dead, there shouldn't be anything holding you back. When you read my offer you'll see that it's more than fair, and you'll also see that it will make you a very rich man."

Sorry, Richard, but two things will hold me back. My integrity and not doing business with someone who is so insensitive he'd call my aunt an old lady after she was murdered. We're miles apart. I just made a decision, and I've decided I'm not going to sell it to you. Still not exactly sure what I'll do with it, but I can guarantee you one thing, you will never own the Robertson Ranch. That I promise you, Aunt Agnes.

"Well, you've given me a lot to think about. I'll get back to you in a few days. My first priority is to find out who murdered my aunt. Again, thanks for coming," Mike said.

"No problem. Sometimes it's a lot easier when a woman isn't involved in a business transaction. Things go a lot smoother when just men are involved. It's always been my experience that old women seem to think differently. When you've had a chance to really examine the plans, I know you're going to want this project to go through. Talk to you in a few days," he said as he walked out to his silver Lexus and quickly drove down the lane.

CHAPTER TWENTY-EIGHT

"Julia, Mike asked me to take a look in the greenhouses. Let's walk over there. Come on everybody."

The parade of Kelly, Julia, Brad, Ella, Olivia, Sam, Lady, and Rebel looked like a line of people and dogs making a pilgrimage as they made their way to the greenhouses. Kelly opened the door of the first one and said, "Oh my gosh! This looks like something out of a gardening magazine. Can you imagine what I could do with fresh produce like this if I had a similar type of greenhouse near the coffee shop? Look, it's even rigged with an automatic drip irrigation system! Agnes wasn't kidding when she said she kept the property up."

Julia looked wistfully at the plants growing in the greenhouse. "I've always wanted to have a greenhouse or a large yard where I could grow fruit trees and vegetables, but living in a condo in San Francisco makes it an impossible dream."

"Let's keep thinking about it, and maybe someday we can make it happen," Brad said. "I'd love it if we could retire to the country and grow all kinds of things. We just can't afford to do it right now. Believe me, no one would like to get out of the big city more than me."

"Based on what you said about wanting to be a cowboy, that's not hard for me to believe," Julia responded.

"Aunt Agnes must have a gardener," Kelly said as they walked into the second greenhouse. "I can't believe she did all the work these greenhouses must require by herself. Someone had to mow the lawn, trim the trees, and tend the plants in the greenhouses." As she stood in front of a wall next to the door she said, "Ah, here's a business card tacked on the wall with the name of the gardener on it. I wonder if he knows she's deceased. I probably better give him a call and let him know. I'm sure Mike will want him to continue working here until he decides what to do with the ranch."

"Has Mike made any decisions yet?" Julia asked.

"No, right now his focus is on finding out who killed Aunt Agnes. When his name is cleared, he's going to have to make a decision. Two people have submitted bids, but I think he's torn over what to do. He doesn't want to see it developed, yet we can't live here and take it over. I honestly don't know what he's got in mind, if anything."

"Dad, now that Grandpa has this house and barn, could we get our own horse and keep it here?"

"Olivia, Grandpa isn't sure what he's going to do with the ranch, but we'll be staying here for another week, and I'm sure Grandpa would be happy to have a little help feeding and grooming Missy. Don't forget that Sam needs some attention too."

"I'm not, Dad. See, I just petted him."

Brad and Julia smiled at each over the girls' heads, happy that the two girls were enjoying themselves so much. "Let's play a game, girls. Let's pretend we lived here. What would you want?" Julia asked.

"Me first, 'cuz I'm oldest," Olivia said. "I'd want my own horse and dog."

"Well, since Missy's in the barn, and you're helping Grandpa feed her, you can pretend she's your horse. And don't forget that Sam slept in the room last night with both of you. That's kind of like having your own dog," Brad said.

"I want the same thing as Olivia," Ella said. "A horse and a dog." Which was absolutely no surprise since Ella always wanted everything her big sister had. In many ways she was a smaller cookie cutter version of her big sister.

"Well," Brad said, "I think my answer to you would be the same as it was for Olivia. Missy and Sam."

"I'd want strawberries, too," Olivia said. "I love strawberries, and we could grow them in that house we were just in, the colored one."

"Sweetheart, it's called a greenhouse. We could probably put a pot of those on our patio and grow them at home, if you'd like."

"Let's do it as soon as we get home."

"It may not happen the second we get home," Julia said, "but I think it's safe for me to promise we can do it very soon."

"I'm sure Grandpa's meeting is over by now. Let's go back to the house and have lunch. I saw a barbeque on the patio, and I'll bet we could talk Grandpa into grilling some hot dogs for us. How about chocolate milk, potato chips, and some strawberries with cream and sugar for dessert? Sound good?"

"Yeah!" Olivia said. "I want lots and lots of strawberries."

"Me, too," Ella mimicked.

*****

After lunch, Kelly said, "Julia, Brad, why don't you two go into town and explore Calico Gold this afternoon? The girls have had a full morning, and after the big lunch they ate, they could probably use a little nap. I've got some things I need to do here at the house while you're gone. Mike, how about you?"

"I really need to go through some of those files I saw in Aunt Agnes' desk. I'd like to be a little more knowledgeable about the ranch now that it's going to be mine. Jim Weaver, the lawyer, called earlier and gave me an accounting of Aunt Agnes' assets. I had no idea she was worth so much. I need to spend some time looking at the accounts and get a better feel for what's going to be mine very soon. Right now I'm simply taking the word of her lawyer, and I don't know anything about the underlying facts and details. Don't get me wrong. I think he's a very good lawyer, but I'm frustrated because he's telling me what I now own, and I don't exactly know what he's talking about."

"Mom, if you're sure it's okay for us to leave, I'd love to explore the town. I think it's utterly charming. Okay with you, Brad?"

"Absolutely. I've always wanted to live in a town like this. Maybe if I see it up close, I'll get rid of that boyhood fantasy of mine about wanting to be a cowboy."

Kelly and the girls headed for the stairs. Sam stood up and followed them. "Olivia, Ella, it looks like the two of you have a friend following you, and I think he wants to take a nap with you."

Sam walked into their bedroom and laid down in the center of the room, directly between the two twin beds. Both of the girls patted him on the head and got into bed for a well-deserved rest.

CHAPTER TWENTY-NINE

After lunch Mike walked into the room his aunt had used as her office and closed the door so he could concentrate in quiet, as he reviewed the financial books and records Aunt Agnes maintained concerning the ranch. Kelly supervised getting the girls started with their nap and then went downstairs to figure out what to fix for dinner.

I think everyone could use a little comfort food tonight. Aunt Agnes kept the refrigerator and pantry so well stocked I can probably find everything I need. I took some steaks out of the freezer this morning, and nothing goes better with steaks than a baked potato with all the trimmings like sour cream, bacon bits, and scallions. I saw some sourdough rolls in the freezer I can defrost, warm, and serve with butter. I'll go out to the greenhouse and get some lettuce to put on salad plates and then cover them with a big tomato salad. Simple yet great! For dessert, I'll make an English trifle. I saw a glass trifle dish in the cupboard. Who can resist the layered combination of strawberries, blueberries, vanilla pudding, and sponge cake, all topped with whipped cream? I'm getting hungry just thinking about it. Anyway, I can make it while the girls are napping. It's easy to fix, and the girls will love more strawberries. Perfect.

She spent the rest of the afternoon in the kitchen. Late in the day Julia and Brad returned. "Mom, have you spent much time in town?" Julia asked.

"No. I've been meaning to, but I always seem to get sidetracked with one thing or another. Did you like it?"

"We absolutely loved it! It's so charming. There are a couple of newer places that don't look like they fit in, but the older buildings on Main Street and some of the shops are simply wonderful. They even have an old ice cream shop, you know, one of those places with the cast iron curlicue chairs painted white with pink and white striped cushions. I had an ice cream cone, but I'd love to go back and have one of their banana splits. I've never seen anything that looked as good as the one I saw being served, plus I don't think many places even serve them anymore."

"Where's Mike?" Brad asked.

"He's been holed up in the office all afternoon. I've been busy in the kitchen, but I don't think he's surfaced."

"Where are the girls?" he asked.

"I put them down for their naps right after you left. They're probably ready to get up by now, but I figured if I wasn't hearing anything from them, that was probably a good thing. You know, kind of like the old saying about letting sleeping dogs lie. There's been a lot of excitement around here, and even though they probably don't understand everything that's going on, they're bound to sense things. I'm sure they were tired."

"I'll go up and check on them. Brad, why don't you see if you can help mom with dinner?" Julia said.

After Julia was out of earshot, Kelly turned to Brad. "Thank you for bringing such happiness to Julia's life. I've never seen her like this. She's absolutely glowing, and she's a natural at being a mother. I don't want to disparage their birth mother, but the girls genuinely seem to think of her as their mother."

"It's interesting. The girls and Julia bonded almost immediately. Having Julia in my life has been wonderful, not only for me, but for the girls as well. Trying to raise two little girls by myself was not easy."

"No, I'm sure it wasn't. You told me Julia's going to adopt them, and I think that's great for everybody. It will make their lives a little more stable, and the one thing I've learned about children is that they need stability. I'm so happy for all of you! Thank you for making my daughter happy. I mean it," she said, touching him lightly on the cheek.

"Think you have that turned around, Kelly. Julia makes all of us happy!"

"Well, whatever or whoever is making everybody happy, I'm glad. Oh Mike, there you are. Brad was just asking about you. Did you get a handle on the financial aspects of the ranch?"

"Yes and no. I was able to figure out exactly what holdings Aunt Agnes had as well as get all the information I need about the property such as when property taxes are due and stuff like that. What I wasn't able to figure out is what in the heck I'm going to do with all of it. That's next on the agenda after we find out who murdered Aunt Agnes. Hear anything from the police chief?"

"Not a word. I'm sure he'll call the minute he finds out anything. He knows how anxious you are. To change the subject, you probably came across the name of the gardener for the ranch in the files you were examining. I found his name in the greenhouse and called him. He knew about your aunt and apologized for not being able to come to the funeral, but he said money is really tight for him, and he couldn't afford to miss a day of work. I told him we understood, and we'd like him to continue to do the gardening for the property. Evidently he comes twice a week. He cuts the lawn, takes care of the flowers and the plants in the greenhouses, and does what's needed in the fruit orchard. He told me he has a helper."

"Thanks. I made a long list of things I need to do concerning the property, and that's one item I can cross off. What's for dinner?"

"You were so good at barbecuing the hot dogs at lunch I decided to let you do it again, only it's going to be steaks, not hot dogs." She told him what she had planned for dinner and mentioned she'd harvested some greenhouse items and that the trifle was in the refrigerator.

"Sounds great. I could use a meal like that after the last few days. Where's Julia?"

"She went up to see if the girls were awake. They'll all probably be down in a few minutes. It's such a beautiful evening, any objections to eating on the patio?"

"No, I'd like that. One of my favorite childhood memories about this place is eating dinner on the patio with my aunt and uncle under the spreading branches of that massive old oak tree that the patio's built around."

"Consider it done," Kelly said.

CHAPTER THIRTY

When they finished dinner, Mike pushed himself back from the large rustic patio table situated under the massive two hundred year old oak tree and said, "Kelly, once again you outdid yourself. That meal was fabulous."

"Wish I could take credit for it, but your aunt had all the ingredients. I think what made it so special was the just-picked freshness of the salad and the strawberries. No store can match that kind of taste."

"Could I have some more dessert?" Olivia asked. "I love the strawberries."

"Me too," parroted Ella.

"You'll have to ask your dad if it's okay. You both ate a lot tonight."

Just then Mike's cell phone rang, and he looked at the monitor. "Excuse me. It's Chief Robbins. Maybe he's got some information for me. I'll take the call in the office."

Brad nodded yes to Kelly, and she got up to get the girls another helping of trifle. As she walked into the kitchen, she tried to hear what Mike was telling the chief, but she couldn't make the words out.

*****

"This is Mike, Chief. Were you able to find out anything?"

"Yes. Are you sitting down?"

"I'm taking it you got a match."

"My friend was able to match the handwriting. I hate to tell you this, but your cousin's handwriting matched the handwriting on the letters."

"You're kidding! And after everything my aunt did for him!"

"That's not all. I told you my friend was one of the foremost handwriting analysts in the country. He was able to determine from the writing that your cousin is a deeply disturbed man who is very, very angry. He feels there is a very good chance your cousin murdered your aunt. I didn't tell him the whole story, but based on what he told me I think you should be very careful and keep away from him. We don't know if he's the one who killed your aunt, but if he is, you could be his next target."

"You're probably right, Chief. Like you, I'm well-trained, and I'll be extra careful until this case is resolved. What's the next step?"

"My deputy and I will go out to his cabin in the morning and ask him some questions. I'm hoping he might be angry enough to admit he wrote the letters, and then I'll have a reason to arrest him. As far as the murder, I'd like him to break down and tell us he did it. Based on the lack of any type of incriminating evidence, that's about our only chance of finding out if he was the one who killed her. Mike, you seem like a man of your word, and I'd like your word that you won't pay him a visit on your own. We'll be out there first thing tomorrow morning, and I'll call you and let you know what we find out."

"I'd like to go out there tonight and confront him, but you've been very fair to me, so yes, I give you my word, I won't go out there tonight. Please thank your friend for me. I'll be curious to hear what

Daniel has to say to you."

"I'll talk to you tomorrow. Have a good evening."

*****

Mike walked out to the patio where Brad, Kelly, and Julia were finishing up the last of the trifle. The girls had gone inside to watch cartoons until it was bed time.

"What did the chief have to say?" Brad asked.

"He found out from his friend that there was a match, and it was my cousin, Daniel Noonan. His friend could also tell from my cousin's handwriting that he's deeply disturbed and very, very angry, which is not a good combination."

"Oh, Mike, I'm so sorry," Kelly said. "It's hard to believe that Daniel sent those letters to your aunt after she'd been supporting him for so many years. He'd be nothing without her. How tragic! What happens now?"

"The chief and his deputy are going out there first thing in the morning. He made me give him my word I wouldn't go out there tonight which I did. Between you and me, what I'd really like to do is go out there with my gun right now and force him to talk. Maybe that's what it will take to get him to admit he killed Aunt Agnes."

"No. Let the chief handle it," Kelly said. "He seems very capable, and that's his job, however I do think we need to be extra careful tonight. Sam's sleeping with the girls, but we'll have Rebel and Lady."

"They're great for protecting, particularly Rebel, but I think it might be wise for both of us to keep our guns on the nightstands tonight," Mike said

Julia's eyes widened. "Are you serious? Do you really think something could happen?"

"I hope not, but when you're dealing with someone who's troubled and angry, that's a very dangerous combination. We already know what he thinks about me inheriting my aunt's estate."

"Mike, I still have the gun Kelly gave me yesterday. I'll have it next to me. The girls are sleeping in the room next to ours. We have a connecting door, and I'll be sure and lock both of the doors that lead to the hall. If you need me for anything, just yell," Brad said standing up from the table. "Julia, let's carry the dishes in and get the girls to bed. Mike, I hope for your sake you resolve this tragic situation tomorrow morning."

"So do I Brad, so do I."

Kelly and Mike finished cleaning up the last of the dinner dishes, let the dogs out, and went upstairs.

"Mike, are you being overly cautious about your cousin? He doesn't seem like a particularly violent man to me, just misguided."

"No, I don't think I'm being the least bit overly cautious, particularly if he was the one who killed Aunt Agnes, and at the moment there's nothing to tell me otherwise. If you hear anything tonight, wake me. Don't try to get up on your own and see what it is. Deal?"

"Deal. Try and get some sleep. If you're going to confront him tomorrow, you need to be rested."

"All right. See you in the morning," he said, kissing her on the cheek and making sure his gun was on the nightstand. The dogs slept at the foot of the bed. He turned off the lamp on the nightstand and laid there for what seemed like hours, tuned into every little sound the old house made during the night. And then he heard it.

CHAPTER THIRTY-ONE

Mike recognized the distinct sound of a glass cutter. When he attended the sheriff's academy there had been a class on different sounds that were made when people were breaking and entering a building, and the sound he now heard matched the sound he'd heard so many years ago. Once you heard it, you never forgot it. Someone was definitely breaking into the house. Rebel heard the sound too. He instantly got up from where he'd been sleeping at the foot of the bed and stood beside Mike, ears alert, a low growl coming from deep in his throat.

Mike gestured towards Kelly who was sleeping peacefully next to him. Rebel walked around the bed and stood next to Kelly as if he could read Mike's mind, guarding her if need be. Mike had had gone to bed dressed in sweat pants and a T-shirt. He swung his long legs off the bed, being careful not to wake up Kelly. He picked up his pistol from where he'd left it on the nightstand. His soft-soled slippers made no sound as he walked over to the door and quietly opened it. He looked back and held his hand up to Rebel, indicating for him to stay where he was, and closed the door.

He walked quietly down the hall to the stairs. The house was dark. After he'd taken several steps, he saw the beam of a flashlight bouncing across the family room on the far side of the stairs. Whoever was breaking in was checking to see if anyone was in the family room before they entered. As the intruder shined his flashlight on the hole the glass cutter had made, Mike saw a gloved hand reach through the opening and turn the inside door lock. The flashlight was focused on where the inside lock was located, giving Mike a few seconds to get to the bottom of the stairs without being seen. The intruder opened the door and stepped inside. In the moonlight that flowed into the room Mike saw a tall man wearing gloves with a dark ski mask covering his face. He was dressed in black jeans and a dark long sleeved t-shirt. He cautiously entered the room and looked around.

Mike stepped behind the open door to the office which allowed him to see the intruder without being seen then he caught his breath. His build and the slight limp he'd gotten from his childhood accident gave the intruder's identity away. It was Daniel Noonan.

Mike flipped the lights on and at the same time shouted, "Put your hands up, or I'll shoot!"

Daniel fired off a wild shot in Mike's direction and ducked down behind a large chair. He yelled at Mike, "You're going to die just like Aunt Agnes did. If I can't have this ranch, you're not going to live to inherit it. I killed her, and now I'm going to kill you. You deserve to die for what your family did to my mother and me. This ranch is rightfully mine. I never got anything from my family, not even a birthday card from my grandparents."

From Mike's position behind the door he saw Kelly and Rebel standing at the top of the stairs with Lady in the background. He waved his arm at Rebel and shouted "Attack." With lightning speed Rebel jumped over the stairway railing and landed squarely on top of Daniel, knocking him down on the floor as he struggled to keep control of his gun. Mike ran over to him, kicked the gun from his hand, and pulled the ski mask off his face. "Don't move, Daniel, or the dog will go for your throat."

Rebel stood on Daniel's chest, all ninety pounds of flesh and bone that seemed as strong as steel holding Daniel flat on his back as he whimpered, "Get the dog off! I can't breathe. Get him off me." As soon as Rebel had leaped over the railing, Lady raced down the stairs, and all Daniel could see were the faces of two very large angry dogs that could rip him apart in seconds if the right command was given.

Kelly had followed Lady down the stairs, and she stood next to Mike, gun in her hand, pointed at Daniel. "Kelly, call 911 and tell the dispatcher I need to be patched through to the chief. Tell her Mike Reynolds needs to talk to him, and that Daniel Noonan has admitted killing my aunt."

In seconds they heard Chief Robbins' voice coming from the speakerphone. "Mike, what's happened?"

"Daniel Noonan broke into the house. He used a glass cutter to cut a hole in one of the window panes of the patio glass door. I heard the sound and surprised him. He said he was going to kill me just like he killed my aunt."

"Did anyone else hear him say that?" the chief asked.

"Yes, Kelly did."

Brad's voice cut in. Kelly and Mike had been so focused on Daniel they hadn't noticed Brad coming down the stairs, two at a time, to reach them. "Chief, I heard him, too. This is Brad. We met at the house yesterday. I'm Mike's son-in-law. I was standing at the top of the stairs, and I heard Daniel admit he killed Mike's aunt, and he also said he was going to kill Mike."

"Mike, I'm assuming you have a gun on him. Correct?"

"Actually, there are three guns on him. Mine, Kelly's, and Brad's. He'll be waiting for you when you get here. By the way, he has two dogs inches from his face that would like nothing better than for me to give them the attack command."

"I'm on my way. I'm calling my deputy, and he'll be there, too. I shouldn't be more than ten minutes. Don't do anything until I get there."

"Don't worry. I think with three guns and two dogs, Daniel Noonan isn't going to try to escape."

"Mom, Brad, what's going on?" Julia asked in a sleepy voice from the top of the stairs.

"We just solved a little problem, honey," Brad said. "Get back in bed and keep the girls upstairs. I'll be up in a little while. Everything's under control."

In minutes they heard the sound of sirens as they drew closer to the house. Car doors swung open, and Chief Robbins yelled, "Mike where are you?"

"We're in the family room."

The chief and his deputy raced into the room, guns drawn. "Chief, get these dogs away from me," Daniel screamed. "I'm having trouble breathing."

"Mike, call the dogs off, and the three of you can put your guns down. Jake and I will take it from here."

"Rebel, Lady, stand down," Mike said in a commanding tone of voice. Rebel jumped off of Daniel's chest and stood by Mike while Lady went to Kelly.

"Daniel, roll over and put your hands behind your back. Jake's going to cuff you. You're not going anywhere except for a ride in a squad car to jail where I'm going to book you for murder and attempted murder."

"Well, Chief, I guess it's over. Daniel admitted he murdered Aunt Agnes, and he tried to kill me," Mike said. "You can see the bullet hole in the wall next to the study door. Think you'll find a match with that bullet and his gun. That's all the evidence you'll need for the attempted murder charge. It pretty much clears the others who were possible suspects for the murder of Aunt Agnes. I'm assuming your friend with the Department of Justice didn't find any other matches."

"No. Not a one. I'd like the three of you to come to the station tomorrow morning and give a statement about what you saw and heard here tonight. It's late or early, however you want to look at it, and I want to get him to the station. Why don't you come in about nine, and we'll do the necessary paperwork then?"

Mike and the chief pulled Daniel to a standing position while Chief Robbins' deputy, Jake, kept his gun on him. "Walk out to the car," the chief said, "and don't think about doing anything funny, or I'll tell Mike to give the dogs the attack command. Understand?"

Daniel muttered something unintelligible and shuffled out the door towards the waiting patrol car, followed by the chief and Jake. Mike watched them put Daniel in the police car then he closed the front door and sagged against it. "Well, I guess this nightmare is over. Now we know who killed my aunt. I still can't believe her own flesh and blood did it." He looked at Kelly. "I thought I closed our bedroom door when I heard the sound of the glass cutter and got out of bed. Did I leave it open?"

"No, you closed it. As soon as you left Rebel put his mouth next to my ear and growled. I saw that you were gone and jumped out of bed. Rebel was already at the bedroom door. I figured he knew what he was doing, so I opened the door, and you know the rest. Evidently he decided you might need some help."

"As a matter of fact I did. If he hadn't come, I don't know what might have happened. Daniel shot at me once and missed, but who knows, he might have hit me with his next shot if it hadn't been for Rebel. Come here, boy," he said, scratching his ears. "Thanks."

Lady stood next to Kelly and looked up at her as if to say, "Hey, what about me? I got there as fast as I could, and I was standing right next to Rebel. At least I deserve an ear scratch, too." Kelly reached down and scratched Lady's ear as if she had understood everything Lady had told her.

"Time for all of us to go back to bed. Maybe we can get a couple of hours of sleep before morning." He looked at Rebel, Lady, Brad, and Kelly, and said, "If it wasn't for all of you, I'm not sure I'd be standing here right now. Thank you."

They walked up the stairs, Mike mentally adding a new item to his "to-do" list - get a new patio glass door.

CHAPTER THIRTY-TWO

"For breakfast, I've fixed a plate of bagels, strawberry jam, whipped cream cheese, and some lox that Aunt Agnes had. You can also have some fresh orange juice," Kelly said.

"Grandma, what's lox?" Olivia asked.

"Fair question. It's a fish that's been prepared a special way. Lots of people like it served in thin slices on their bagels. You might try it and see what you think."

"No," Olivia said, "I don't like fish."

"Me neither," aped Ella.

"Girls, that's probably why Grandma put the strawberry jam and cream cheese out. Bagels with that on it will taste great."

"Julia, the three of us need to go to the police station to give our statements about last night. Why don't you take the girls to the barn and comb Missy? I'm sure Sam would love to go with you," Brad said.

I'm glad the girls slept through the commotion last night, and we can get a new glass door installed today. Shouldn't be that difficult. I'll call as soon as I get back from the police station. With their mother dying from a cocaine overdose, they've had enough tragedy in their young lives. They don't need to know that someone broke in last night intent on killing their grandfather, Mike thought as he, Kelly, and Brad got in his car and headed for the police station.

An hour later they returned from giving their official statements. Daniel was going to be arraigned that afternoon, and Chief Robbins felt confident he would go to prison for a long time, if not life. Judges and juries don't look too kindly on murder and attempted murder. Chief Robbins told them they would need to testify at Daniel's trial, if it came to that. With as much strong evidence as there was against him, there was a good chance his public defender would try for a plea bargain.

"Kelly, Brad, I need to make some phone calls," Mike said, "and then I'd like to have a little talk with both of you as well as Julia later today. I don't know what you have planned for the rest of the day, but carve a little time out for me. I'll be in the office."

Kelly heard Mike talking to several people on the phone, but she couldn't make out what he was saying. It was unlike Mike not to share what he was doing with her, and she couldn't help but be more than a little curious. She made sandwiches for lunch for everyone and took a plate into the office for Mike.

"Thanks, Kelly," Mike said smiling.

"You look like the weight of the world has been lifted from your shoulders."

"It has, sweetheart, believe me, it has. Any chance we could have that little meeting I mentioned earlier in about an hour? I have one more phone call to make, and then I'd really like to talk to the three of you. Any chance you could find some kid's show on television for the girls to watch while we're talking?"

"I don't know about that, but Julia said she brought a couple of movies on her iPad for the girls, and that should work. Shall we join you here in the office in about an hour?"

"Yes, please, and Kelly, I think you're going to be happy with what I have to say."

"Mike, if you're happy I'm happy, but I have no clue what's going on."

"That's okay, just trust me. Deal?"

"Deal."

*****

An hour later Kelly, Brad, and Julia walked into the office, while the girls were in the family room, happily watching their favorite movie on Julia's iPad. "Here we are, Mike, what's up?" Brad asked.

"Please, sit down. As you know, I've been trying to figure out what I'm going to do with all of this – the ranch, the house, and the money – ever since I found out I was the sole beneficiary named in Aunt Agnes' Will. I honestly didn't know where to start. Kelly and I have a good life in Cedar Bay. She loves owning and managing Kelly's Koffee Shop, and I love being the Beaver County Sheriff. May sound pretty schmaltzy, but that's the truth."

"Mike, no one needs to apologize for being happy living in a small town. Matter of fact, wish I could," Brad said.

"Well, you just might," he said to Brad who had a surprised look on his face, clearly befuddled by Mike's words. "Here's what I've been dealing with. Aunt Agnes had this property and the house as well as a lot of other assets. She'd invested very well, and her estate is worth about twenty million dollars including the ranch and the house. I'd like to make a proposition to you, and before you answer, please hear me out.

"I'm the last of the legitimate relatives of Aunt Agnes. Yes, Daniel is her nephew, but for numerous reasons which all of us know, I'm taking him out of the equation. Anyway, if I were to keep the property, there is no other heir for me to leave it to, since I've never had children. It would have to be sold when I died. I could choose to sell it now, but Aunt Agnes didn't want to sell the ranch, and I want to respect her wishes."

"So you're kind of back to square one, aren't you, Mike?" Kelly asked.

"Not really. Julia, I would like to adopt you. I've talked to Jim Weaver, Aunt Agnes' attorney, and he tells me that while adult adoptions are somewhat uncommon, they are legal. I have several reasons for wanting to do this. I'd like you and Brad and the girls to live here. Brad, you could run cattle here or do whatever you wanted to do with the property other than sell it or develop it. You both have said you'd like to live in a small town. The girls have indicated they'd love to live here. I was thinking you would live here rent free, and I would pay you an annual fee for managing the property. At my death, the property would go to you, Julia. After the adoption you would legally be my daughter, and by leaving the ranch to you it would stay in the family. I would hope you would leave it to one or both of the girls when you die, and the family lineage and ownership of the Robertson Ranch would continue to remain in the family. Oh, I almost forgot. I'd like you to keep Sam for the girls. He certainly seems to be taken with them. Of course Missy would continue to stay here."

Kelly looked over at Julia who was sitting in shock, her mouth open, and tears beginning to stream down her face. "Oh, Mike, your offer to adopt me is the biggest compliment I've ever had. I would be honored to legally become your daughter. Brad, can we do it?"

"Absolutely. I don't even need to think about it. We'll go back to San Francisco, sell our condo, and move here. This is like a dream come true, Mike. I've wanted to leave San Francisco forever. Maybe I could set up a psychology practice here in town. Who knows? We can never thank you enough."

Mike looked at Kelly. "I know you're wondering about Cash, and if Julia gets the ranch, is this is fair to him? I'm prepared to give Cash an amount equal to what the ranch is worth. He has his career in the military service, and he isn't in a position to move here. Julia and Brad are. Is that all right with you? I probably should have cleared my proposal with you first. What do you think about it?"

"I say it's the most generous thing I've ever seen or heard. On behalf of Cash, thank you," Kelly said.

"Brad, I had a long conversation with John Wilson this morning about the stream. I'm going to open the dam. He's a good man, and he's desperate for water for his cattle. I know my uncle wanted to live completely self-sufficiently, but I think if he knew how critical the water shortage has become, he'd agree to open the dam. To say that John was grateful would be the understatement of the year. Actually, I feel really good about it. It was the right thing to do."

"I'm glad you did that, Mike. He seems like he has best the interests of his family and his animals at heart, and I'm sure he's thrilled about your decision," Brad said.

"I left a message for Richard Martin informing him I wouldn't be selling the property to him. I'm sure it won't make him happy, but from the brief time I spent with him, I'm certain he has other places where he's looking. Of course, since John's getting the dam opened, he won't be selling to Richard either. Can't say I feel too sorry for Richard. I didn't trust or like that man from the get go."

"Mike, that takes care of the house and the property, but what about the rest of Agnes' assets?" Kelly asked.

"I'm getting to that. In about ten minutes Huston Brooks will be coming here. It's very hard to beat an incumbent whose already been elected to office three times, and I think there's a very good chance he's going to lose the election to Judge Lane.

"I'm going to offer him the position of being the Executive Director of the Agnes Johnson Calico Gold Preservation Trust. I'll put the rest of her assets into a special trust, and he can oversee it. I envision it being for the purpose of keeping Calico Gold free from outsiders coming in and taking over the town. He and my aunt were very close, and I would make it worth his while, financially. It's something I think would make her happy."

"That's a wonderful idea. Do you think he'll do it?" Brad asked.

"I don't know. We'll find out fairly soon. Oh, Kelly, there is one more thing. Every time we try to take a honeymoon it seems like it gets cut short. First of all, Jesse was murdered and then Aunt Agnes. I think it would be a good idea for you and me to take a real honeymoon. How does Italy sound? I even looked on the Internet, and there's a cooking school not far from Florence that I think would be fun for us to attend. We could go there and then spend a couple of days exploring ..."

Before he could get the word "Italy" out of his mouth, Kelly had jumped out of her chair and ran over to him, hugging and kissing him. "Well, if that's the reception the idea gets, I should have done it a long time ago," Mike said, laughing.

"Wow! You've thought of everything. We need to make some plans about Italy and Cash and..."

Before she could finish, they heard a car approaching. Kelly looked out the window and said, "Huston's here. Why don't we go in the other room? It would probably be best if you talked to him privately."

"Thanks. I think that's a good idea. I'll answer the door. By the way, Kelly, the man who's going to replace the patio glass door should be here any minute. Would you take care of it? I've already written a check out for him."

"Of course."

Julia and Brad went upstairs to tell the girls the news. A moment later Kelly heard Olivia and Ella's joyful voices screaming, "Really, really? We can have a horse? Each one of us? And Sam can live with us?"

*****

While Mike met with Huston, Kelly made sure the glass door was properly installed and the new lock worked. Just as the repairman was leaving, Mike opened the door to the office. "Would you come in here for a moment?" he asked, smiling broadly at her.

"Kelly, I want you to be the first to congratulate the Executive Director of the Agnes Johnson Calico Gold Preservation Trust."

"Huston, I'm so glad you decided to do this. You're perfect for it, and I know it would make Aunt Agnes happy. You have my absolute congratulations and support."

"Thanks, Kelly. I certainly wasn't planning on this happening when I got up this morning, but it actually comes at a good time. Several of my clients have begged me not to close my law practice, and my wife is not very fond of politics. With this opportunity, I can keep my practice, my wife will be happy, and I'll feel like I'm doing something good for Calico Gold. Plus, there's a very good chance I would have lost the election to Judge Lane. She definitely has a number of people in her pocket who want to keep her in office. I still think she's got some baggage, actually a lot of baggage, but I don't think this is the right time for me to take her on. Who knows? Maybe I will at a later date. Mike, thanks for your faith in me. I'd like to get together with you and the banker in town and figure out how we should set this up. I can do the legal part, but I want to make sure the bank is on board as well. Are you planning on staying here for a few more days?"

"Yes, I still need to take care of some loose ends, but as soon as they're finished, Kelly and I need to get back to Cedar Bay and start planning our trip to Italy. Deal, Kelly?"

"Deal!"

RECIPES

TOMATO SALAD

Ingredients

4 large ripe tomatoes
½ tsp. salt
4 garlic cloves
1 tbsp. olive oil
4 lettuce leaves

Directions

Core tomatoes and finely chop. Put the tomatoes in a colander and drain. Finely chop garlic. Combine drained tomatoes, garlic, and salt in mixing bowl. Stir in olive oil. Chill in refrigerator for at least one hour. If desired, drain in colander again to get rid of excess liquid (salt draws liquid out of tomatoes) and spoon over lettuce leaves.

SUPER EASY ENGLISH TRIFLE

Ingredients

6 cups sponge cake, torn into pieces (about 1" in size)
1 basket strawberries
1 basket blueberries

1 basket raspberries
3 bananas peeled and sliced in 1/4" rounds
3 tbsp. raisins
3 ¼ oz. package vanilla pudding mix
2 cups milk
1 8 oz. carton whipping cream
2 tbsp. slivered almonds
3 tbsp. powdered sugar, sifted
Optional: 1 ½ oz. brandy

Directions

Chill mixing bowl and beaters of electric mixer in freezer. If desired, sprinkle brandy over sponge cake pieces.

In a separate bowl, mix pudding mix and milk together according to package instructions. Place 1/3 of the sponge cake pieces in large bowl that is 10 – 12 inches deep. (If you have a large glass bowl or trifle bowl, use it for a nice presentation.) In a separate bowl gently mix blueberries, bananas, strawberries, raspberries and raisins together, and place 1/3 of them over sponge cake. Smooth 1/3 pudding mix over the fruit mixture. Repeat layers as above until you have assembled three layers in the bowl.

Take the mixing bowl and beaters out of the freezer and pour in the whipping cream and powdered sugar. Beat with an electric mixer until whipped cream holds stiff peaks.

Spread whipped cream on top of the last layer of pudding mix. Sprinkle the slivered almonds on top of the whipped cream. Cover with plastic wrap and refrigerate until ready to serve. Enjoy!

Note: Feel free to experiment with different seasonal fruit.

APRICOT BREAD

Ingredients

1 cup dried apricots
1/2 cup water
1 cup sugar
1 egg
1/2 cup orange juice
2 cups flour
1/2 tsp. salt
1/4 tsp. baking soda
2 tsp. baking powder
Optional: 1/2 cup chopped walnuts

Directions

Preheat oven to 350 degrees. Cut apricots up into small bite-size pieces and soak in water for 30 minutes.

Mix rest of ingredients together in a bowl. Drain the apricots and add to the mixture in the bowl. Place in greased and floured loaf pan for 20 minutes before baking. Bake for 55-60 minutes.

BIG SMILE CAKE

Cake Mix Ingredients

1 box of yellow or lemon cake mix
3 eggs
½ cup oil
1 cup water

Rest of Ingredients

2 lbs. ricotta cheese
1 cup sugar
2 eggs

3 tbsp. powdered sugar

Directions

Preheat oven to 350 degrees. Prepare cake mix according to directions on box and place in lightly oiled 9" x 13" Pyrex glass pan. Mix ricotta cheese, sugar, and eggs together. Spread evenly over cake mix. Bake 1 hour. When cool sprinkle powdered sugar on top.

STUFFED BAKED JUMBO PASTA SHELLS

Ingredients

4 mild Italian sausages
1 box jumbo pasta shells
15 oz. ricotta cheese
1 cup shredded parmesan cheese, divided in half
1 ½ cups shredded mozzarella cheese, divided in half
2 egg whites
10 oz. box frozen spinach, thawed with moisture pressed out
½ tsp. garlic powder
½ tsp. onion salt
1 tsp. Kosher salt (for pasta water)
½ tsp. salt
½ tsp. pepper
2 tsp. chopped fresh parsley
3 ½ cups prepared marinara sauce
1 cup water

Directions

Preheat oven to 350 degrees. Put the sausages on a microwave-safe plate, place a paper towel over them, and microwave for 8 – 10 minutes on high, until cooked through. Let cool and cut in half lengthwise, remove casings and discard. Cut into bite-size pieces.

Fill large pot with water and bring to a boil, add Kosher salt and the pasta. Cook 10 minutes. Drain but don't rinse.

In large bowl place chopped sausage, ricotta cheese, ½ of mozzarella cheese, ½ of parmesan cheese, egg whites, garlic powder, spinach, onion salt, salt, pepper, and parsley. Stir until all ingredients are thoroughly combined.

In another large bowl combine marinara sauce and water. Pour 1 3/4 cups of mixture in bottom of 9" x 13" Pyrex pan.

Fill pasta shells with cheese and sausage mixture and place on top of marinara sauce. Pour the rest of the marina sauce over the assembled shells. Sprinkle remaining mozzarella cheese and parmesan cheese on top of shells and sauce.

Cover with tin foil, place in oven and bake for 30 minutes. Remove tin foil and cook for an additional 15 minutes. Let cool for five minutes and serve. Enjoy!

ABOUT THE AUTHOR

Dianne lives in Huntington Beach, California with her husband Tom, a former California State Senator, and her boxer puppy, Kelly. Her passions are cooking and dogs, so whenever she has a little free time, you can find her in the kitchen or in the back yard throwing a ball for Kelly. She is a frequent contributor to the Huffington Post.

Her other award winning books include:

Cedar Bay Cozy Mystery Series
Kelly's Koffee Shop, Murder at Jade Cove, White Cloud Retreat, Marriage and Murder, Murder in the Pearl District

Liz Lucas Cozy Mystery Series
Murder in Cottage #6, Murder & Brandy Boy

Coyote Series
Blue Coyote Motel, Coyote in Provence, Cornered Coyote

Website: www.dianneharman.com
Blog: www.dianneharman.com/blog
Email: dianne@dianneharman.com

Newsletter
To keep abreast with her latest releases kindly go to www.dianneharman.com and sign up for her newsletter. Thank you.

Made in the USA
Charleston, SC
19 November 2015